SLACPID PURSUES THE WRAITH

# Tales of Romance

Anonymous Author

*Originally Published by*
LONGMANS, GREEN AND CO.
1919

# Contents

**THE STORY OF ROBIN HOOD.**     5

PART I. . . . . . . . . . . . . . . . . . . . . . . . . . . . . 5

PART II. . . . . . . . . . . . . . . . . . . . . . . . . . . . 7

Robin Hood's meeting with Little John. . . . . . . . . . . . . . 9

PART III. . . . . . . . . . . . . . . . . . . . . . . . . . . 11

PART IV. . . . . . . . . . . . . . . . . . . . . . . . . . . . 15

The Knight repays the four hundred pounds . . . . . . . . . . . . 17

PART V. . . . . . . . . . . . . . . . . . . . . . . . . . . . 19

PART VI. . . . . . . . . . . . . . . . . . . . . . . . . . . . 21

PART VII. . . . . . . . . . . . . . . . . . . . . . . . . . . 23

When the Sheriff saw his own vessels his appetite went from him . . . . 25

PART VIII. . . . . . . . . . . . . . . . . . . . . . . . . . . 27

Friar Tuck upsets Robin Hood . . . . . . . . . . . . . . . . . 29

PART IX. . . . . . . . . . . . . . . . . . . . . . . . . . . . 31

PART X. . . . . . . . . . . . . . . . . . . . . . . . . . . . 33

PART XI. . . . . . . . . . . . . . . . . . . . . . . . . . . . 35

There is pith in your arm said Robin Hood . . . . . . . . . . . . 39

PART XII. . . . . . . . . . . . . . . . . . . . . . . . . . . 41

PART XIII. . . . . . . . . . . . . . . . . . . . . . . . . . . 43

Robin Hood shoots his last arrow . . . . . . . . . . . . . . . . . . 45

## WAYLAND THE SMITH.     49

PART I. . . . . . . . . . . . . . . . . . . . . . . . . . . . . . . . 49

PART II. . . . . . . . . . . . . . . . . . . . . . . . . . . . . . . 51

The three women by the stream . . . . . . . . . . . . . . . 55

PART III. . . . . . . . . . . . . . . . . . . . . . . . . . . . . . . 57

PART IV. . . . . . . . . . . . . . . . . . . . . . . . . . . . . . . 59

PART V. . . . . . . . . . . . . . . . . . . . . . . . . . . . . . . 61

PART VI. . . . . . . . . . . . . . . . . . . . . . . . . . . . . . . 63

PART VII. . . . . . . . . . . . . . . . . . . . . . . . . . . . . . 65

PART VIII. . . . . . . . . . . . . . . . . . . . . . . . . . . . . 67

PART IX. . . . . . . . . . . . . . . . . . . . . . . . . . . . . . . 69

PART X. . . . . . . . . . . . . . . . . . . . . . . . . . . . . . . 71

Wayland mocked by the Queen and Banvilda . . . . . . . . . . . . . 73

PART XI. . . . . . . . . . . . . . . . . . . . . . . . . . . . . . . 75

PART XII. . . . . . . . . . . . . . . . . . . . . . . . . . . . . . 77

The merman warns Banvilda in vain . . . . . . . . . . . . . . . . 79

The Chariot of Freya . . . . . . . . . . . . . . . . . . . . . . . . 81

## SOME ADVENTURES OF WILLIAM SHORT NOSE.     85

PART I. . . . . . . . . . . . . . . . . . . . . . . . . . . . . . . . 85

PART II. . . . . . . . . . . . . . . . . . . . . . . . . . . . . . . 87

Vivian's last confession . . . . . . . . . . . . . . . . . . . . . 89

| | |
|---|---|
| PART III. | 91 |
| PART IV. | 93 |
| The Captives—William Short-nose rides to the rescue | 95 |
| PART V. | 97 |
| PART VI. | 99 |
| PART VII. | 101 |
| The Lady Alix stays the wrath of William Shortnose | 103 |
| PART VIII. | 105 |
| PART IX. | 107 |
| Alix kisses Rainouart | 109 |
| PART X. | 111 |
| PART XI. | 113 |
| The Lady Gibourc with Rainouart in the kitchen | 115 |
| PART XII. | 117 |
| Rainouart stops the cowards | 119 |
| PART XIII. | 121 |
| PART XIV. | 123 |

## THE SWORD EXCALIBUR 127

| | |
|---|---|
| Arthur meets the Lady of the Lake and gets the sword Excalibur | 129 |

## HOW GRETTIR THE STRONG BECAME AN OUTLAW. 133

| | |
|---|---|
| I | 133 |
| Grettir overthrows Thorir Redbeard | 137 |

**DEATH OF GRETTIR THE STRONG.** 141

SLAGFID PURSUES THE WRAITH.

# THE STORY OF ROBIN HOOD.

# PART I.

Many hundreds of years ago, when the Plantagenets were kings, England was so covered with woods, that a squirrel was said to be able to hop from tree to tree from the Severn to the Humber.

It must have been very different to look at from the country we travel through now; but still there were roads that ran from north to south and from east to west, for the use of those who wished to leave their homes, and at certain times of the year these roads were thronged with people.

Pilgrims going to some holy shrine passed along, merchants taking their wares to Court, Abbots and Bishops ambling by on palfreys to bear their part in the King's Council, and, more frequently still, a solitary Knight, seeking adventures.

Besides the broad roads there were small tracks and little green paths, and these led to clumps of low huts, where dwelt the peasants, charcoal-burners, and ploughmen, and here and there some larger clearing than usual told that the house of a yeoman was near.

Now and then as you passed through the forest you might ride by a splendid abbey, and catch a glimpse of monks in long black or white gowns, fishing in the streams and rivers that abound in this part of England, or casting nets in the fish ponds which were in the midst of the abbey gardens. Or you might chance to see a castle with round turrets and high battlements, circled by strong walls, and protected by a moat full of water.

This was the sort of England into which the famous Robin Hood was born. We do not know anything about him, who he was, or where he lived, or what evil deed he had done to put him beyond the King's grace. For he was an outlaw, and any man might kill him and never pay penalty for it.

But, outlaw or not, the poor people loved him and looked on him as their friend, and many a stout fellow came to join him, and led a merry life in the greenwood, with moss and fern for bed, and for meat the King's deer, which it was death to slay.

Peasants of all sorts, tillers of the land, yeomen, and as some say Knights, went on their ways freely, for of them Robin took no toll; but lordly churchmen with money-bags well filled, or proud Bishops with their richly dressed followers, trembled as they drew near to Sherwood Forest—who was to know whether behind every tree there did not lurk Robin Hood or some of his men?

# PART II.

*THE COMING OF LITTLE JOHN.*

One day Robin was walking alone in the wood, and reached a river which was spanned by a very narrow bridge, over which one man only could pass. In the midst stood a stranger, and Robin bade him go back and let him go over. "I am no man of yours," was all the answer Robin got, and in anger he drew his bow and fitted an arrow to it.

"Would you shoot a man who has no arms but a staff?" asked the stranger in scorn; and with shame Robin laid down his bow, and unbuckled an oaken stick at his side. "We will fight till one of us falls into the water," he said; and fight they did, till the stranger planted a blow so well that Robin rolled over into the river.

PART II.

# Robin Hood's meeting with Little John.

"You are a brave soul," said he, when he had waded to land, and he blew a blast with his horn which brought fifty good fellows, clad in green, to the little bridge.

"Have you fallen into the river that your clothes are wet?" asked one; and Robin made answer, "No, but this stranger, fighting on the bridge, got the better of me, and tumbled me into the stream."

At this the foresters seized the stranger, and would have ducked him had not their leader bade them stop, and begged the stranger to stay with them and make one of themselves. "Here is my hand," replied the stranger, "and my heart with it. My name, if you would know it, is John Little."

"That must be altered," cried Will Scarlett; "we will call a feast, and henceforth, because he is full seven feet tall and round the waist at least an ell, he shall be called Little John."

And thus it was done; but at the feast Little John, who always liked to know exactly what work he had to do, put some questions to Robin Hood. "Before I join hands with you, tell me first what sort of life is this you lead? How am I to know whose goods I shall take, and whose I shall leave? Whom I shall beat, and whom I shall refrain from beating?"

And Robin answered: "Look that you harm not any tiller of the ground, nor any yeoman of the greenwood—no, nor no Knight nor Squire, unless you have heard him ill spoken of. But if Bishops or Archbishops come your way, see that you spoil *them*, and mark that you always hold in your mind the High Sheriff of Nottingham."

This being settled, Robin Hood declared Little John to be second in command to himself among the brotherhood of the forest, and the new outlaw never forgot to "hold in his mind" the High Sheriff of Nottingham, who was the bitterest enemy the foresters had.

Robin Hood, however, had no liking for a company of idle men about him, and he at once sent off Little John and Will Scarlett to the great road known as Watling Street, with orders to hide among the trees and wait till some adventure might come to them; and if they took captive Earl or Baron, Abbot or Knight, he was to be brought unharmed back to Robin Hood.

But all along Watling Street the road was bare; white and hard it lay in the sun, without the tiniest cloud of dust to show that a rich company might be coming: east and west the land lay still.

# PART III.

*LITTLE JOHN'S FIRST ADVENTURE.*

At length, just where a side path turned into the broad highway, there rode a Knight, and a sorrier man than he never sat a horse on summer day. One foot only was in the stirrup, the other hung carelessly by his side; his head was bowed, the reins dropped loose, and his horse went on as he would. At so sad a sight the hearts of the outlaws were filled with pity, and Little John fell on his knees and bade the Knight welcome in the name of his master.

"Who is your master?" asked the Knight.

"Robin Hood," answered Little John.

"I have heard much good of him," replied the Knight, "and will go with you gladly."

Then they all set off together, tears running down the Knight's cheeks as he rode, but he said nothing, neither was anything said to him. And in this wise they came to Robin Hood.

"Welcome, Sir Knight," cried he, "and thrice welcome, for I waited to break my fast till you or some other had come to me."

"God save you, good Robin," answered the Knight, and after they had washed themselves in the stream, they sat down to dine off bread and wine, with flesh of the King's deer, and swans and pheasants. "Such a dinner have I not had for three weeks and more," said the Knight. "And if I ever come again this way, good Robin, I will give you as fine a dinner as you have given me."

"I thank you," replied Robin, "my dinner is always welcome; still, I am none so greedy but I can wait for it. But before you go, pay me, I pray you, for the food which you have had. It was never the custom for a yeoman to pay for a Knight."

"My bag is empty," said the Knight, "save for ten shillings only."

"Go, Little John, and look in his wallet," said Robin, "and, Sir Knight, if in truth you have no more, not one penny will I take; nay, I will give you all that you shall need."

So Little John spread out the Knight's mantle, and opened the bag, and therein lay ten shillings and naught besides.

"What tidings, Little John?" cried his master.

"Sir, the Knight speaks truly," said Little John.

"Then fill a cup of the best wine and tell me, Sir Knight, whether it is your own ill doings which have brought you to this sorry pass."

"For an hundred years my fathers have dwelt in the forest," answered the Knight, "and four hundred pounds might they spend yearly. But within two years misfortune has befallen me, and my wife and children also."

"How did this evil come to pass?" asked Robin.

"Through my own folly," answered the Knight, "and because of the great love I bore my son, who would never be guided of my counsel, and slew, ere he was twenty years old, a Knight of Lancaster and his Squire. For their deaths I had to pay a large sum, which I could not raise without giving my lands in pledge to the rich Abbot of St. Mary's. If I cannot bring him the money by a certain day they will be lost to me for ever."

"What is the sum?" asked Robin. "Tell me truly."

"It is four hundred pounds," said the Knight.

"And what will you do if you lose your lands?" asked Robin again.

"Hide myself over the sea," said the Knight, "and bid farewell to my friends and country. There is no better way open to me."

At this tears fell from his eyes, and he turned him to depart. "Good day, my friend," he said to Robin, "I cannot pay you what I should——" But Robin held him fast. "Where *are* your friends?" asked he.

"Sir, they have all forsaken me since I became poor, and they turn away their heads if we meet upon the road, though when I was rich they were ever in my castle."

When Little John and Will Scarlett and the rest heard this, they wept for very shame and fury, and Robin bade them fill a cup of the best wine, and give it to the Knight.

"Have you no one who would stay surety for you?" said he.

"None," answered the Knight, "but only Our Lady, who has never yet failed to help me."

"You speak well," said Robin, "and you, Little John, go to my treasure chest, and bring me thence four hundred pounds. And be sure you count it truly."

So Little John went, and Will Scarlett, and they brought back the money.

"Sir," said Little John, when Robin had counted it and found it no more nor no less, "look at his clothes, how thin they are! You have stores of garments, green and scarlet, in your coffers—no merchant in England can boast the like. I will measure some out with my bow." And thus he did.

"Master," spoke Little John again, "there is still something else. You must give him a horse, that he may go as beseems his quality to the Abbey."

"Take the grey horse," said Robin, "and put a new saddle on it, and take likewise a good palfrey and a pair of boots, with gilt spurs on them. And as it would be a shame for a Knight to ride by himself on this errand, I will lend you Little John as Squire—perchance he may stand you in yeoman's stead."

"When shall we meet again?" asked the Knight.

"This day twelve months," said Robin, "under the greenwood tree."

Then the Knight rode on his way, with Little John behind him, and as he went he thought of Robin Hood and his men, and blessed them for the goodness they had shown towards him.

"To-morrow," he said to Little John, "I must be at the Abbey of St. Mary, which is in the city of York, for if I am but so much as a day late my lands are lost forever, and though I were to bring the money I should not be suffered to redeem them."

# PART IV.

Now the Abbot had been counting the days as well as the Knight, and the next morning he said to his monks: "This day year there came a Knight and borrowed of me four hundred pounds, giving his lands in surety. And if he come not to pay his debt ere midnight tolls they will be ours for ever."

"It is full early yet," answered the Prior, "he may still be coming."

"He is far beyond the sea," said the Abbot, "and suffers from hunger and cold. How is he to get here?"

"It were a shame," said the Prior, "for you to take his lands. And you do him much wrong if you drive such a hard bargain."

"He is dead or hanged," spake a fat-headed monk who was the cellarer, "and we shall have his four hundred pounds to spend on our gardens and our wines," and he went with the Abbot to attend the court of justice, wherein the Knight's lands would be declared forfeited by the High Justiciar.

"If he come not this day," cried the Abbot, rubbing his hands, "if he come not this day, they will be ours."

"He will not come yet," said the Justiciar, but he knew not that the Knight was already at the outer gate, and Little John with him.

"Welcome, Sir Knight," said the porter. "The horse that you ride is the noblest that ever I saw. Let me lead them both to the stable, that they may have food and rest."

"They shall not pass these gates," answered the Knight sternly, and he entered the hall alone, where the monks were sitting at meat, and knelt down and bowed to them.

"I have come back, my lord," he said to the Abbot, who had just returned from the court. "I have come back this day as I promised."

"Have you brought my money?" was all the Abbot said.

"Not a penny," answered the Knight, who wished to see how the Abbot would treat him.

"Then what do you here without it?" cried the Abbot in angry tones.

"I have come to pray you for a longer day," answered the Knight meekly.

"The day was fixed and cannot be gainsaid," replied the Justiciar; but the Knight only begged that he would stand his friend and help him in his strait. "I am with the Abbot," was all the Justiciar would answer.

"Good Sir Abbot, be my friend," prayed the Knight again, "and give me one chance more to get the money and free my lands. I will serve you day and night till I have four hundred pounds to redeem them."

But the Abbot only vowed that the money must be paid that day or the lands be forfeited.

The Knight stood up straight and tall: "It is well," said he, "to prove one's friends against the hour of need," and he looked the Abbot full in the face, and the Abbot felt uneasy, he did not know why, and hated the Knight more than ever. "Out of my hall, false Knight!" cried he, pretending to a courage which he did not feel. But the Knight stayed where he was, and answered him, "You lie, Abbot. Never was I false, and that I have shown in jousts and in tourneys."

"Give him two hundred pounds more," said the Justiciar to the Abbot, "and keep the lands yourself."

"No, by Heaven!" answered the Knight, "not if you offered me a thousand pounds would I do it! Neither Justiciar, Abbot, nor Monk shall be heir of mine." Then he strode up to a table and emptied out four hundred pounds. "Take your gold, Sir Abbot, which you lent to me a year agone. Had you but received me civilly, I would have paid you something more.

# The Knight repays the four hundred pounds

"Sir Abbot, and ye men of law,
　Now have I kept my day!
　Now shall I have my land again,
　For aught that you may say."

So he passed out of the hall singing merrily, leaving the Abbot staring silently after him, and rode back to his house, where his wife met him at the gate.

　"Welcome, my lord," said his lady,
　"Sir, lost is all your good."
　"Be merry, dame," said the Knight,
　"And pray for Robin Hood.
　"But for his kindness, we had been beggars."

# PART V.

After this the Knight dwelt at home, looking after his lands and saving his money carefully, till the four hundred pounds lay ready for Robin Hood. Then he bought a hundred bows and a hundred arrows, and every arrow was an ell long, and had a head of silver and peacock's feathers. And clothing himself in white and red, and with a hundred men in his train, he set off to Sherwood Forest.

On the way he passed an open space near a bridge where there was a wrestling, and the Knight stopped and looked, for he himself had taken many a prize in that sport. Here the prizes were such as to fill any man with envy; a fine horse, saddled and bridled, a great white bull, a pair of gloves, a ring of bright red gold, and a pipe of wine.

There was not a yeoman present who did not hope to win one of them. But when the wrestling was over, the yeoman who had beaten them all was a man who kept apart from his fellows, and was said to think much of himself.

Therefore the men grudged him his skill, and set upon him with blows, and would have killed him, had not the Knight, for love of Robin Hood, taken pity on him, while his followers fought with the crowd, and would not suffer them to touch the prizes a better man had won.

When the wrestling was finished the Knight rode on, and there under the greenwood tree, in the place appointed, he found Robin Hood and his merry men waiting for him, according to the tryst that they had fixed last year:—

"God save thee, Robin Hood,
And all this company."
"Welcome be thou, gentle Knight,
And right welcome to me.
"Hast thou thy land again?" said Robin,
"Truth then tell thou me."
"Yea, for God," said the Knight,
"And that thank I God and thee.
"Have here four hundred pounds," said the Knight,
"The which you lent to me;
And here are also twenty marks
For your courtesie."

But Robin would not take the money. A miracle had happened, he said, and Our Lady had paid it to him, and shame would it be for him to take it twice over.

Then he noticed for the first time the bows and arrows which the Knight had brought, and asked what they were. "A poor present to you," answered the Knight, and Robin, who would not be outdone, sent Little John once more to his treasury, and bade him bring forth four hundred pounds, which was given to the Knight.

After that they parted, in much love, and Robin prayed the Knight if he were in any strait "to let him know at the greenwood tree, and while there was any gold there he should have it".

# PART VI.

*HOW LITTLE JOHN BECAME THE SHERIFF'S SERVANT.*

Meanwhile the High Sheriff of Nottingham proclaimed a great shooting-match in a broad open space, and Little John was minded to try his skill with the rest. He rode through the forest, whistling gaily to himself, for well he knew that not one of Robin Hood's men could send an arrow as straight as he, and he felt little fear of anyone else.

When he reached the trysting place he found a large company assembled, the Sheriff with them, and the rules of the match were read out: where they were to stand, how far the mark was to be, and how that three tries should be given to every man.

Some of the shooters shot near the mark, some of them even touched it, but none but Little John split the slender wand of willow with every arrow that flew from his bow.

At this sight the Sheriff of Nottingham swore that Little John was the best archer that ever he had seen, and asked him who he was and where he was born, and vowed that if he would enter his service he would give twenty marks a year to so good a bowman.

Little John, who did not wish to confess that he was one of Robin Hood's men and an outlaw, said his name was Reynold Greenleaf, and that he was in the service of a Knight, whose leave he must get before he became the servant of any man.

This was given heartily by the Knight, and Little John bound himself to the Sheriff for the space of twelve months, and was given a good white horse to ride on whenever he went abroad. But for all that he did not like his bargain, and made up his mind to do the Sheriff, who was hated of the outlaws, all the mischief he could.

His chance came on a Wednesday when the Sheriff always went hunting, and Little John lay in bed till noon, when he grew hungry. Then he got up, and told the steward that he wanted some dinner. The steward answered he should have nothing till the Sheriff came home, so Little John grumbled and left him, and sought out the butler.

Here he was no more successful than before; the butler just went to the buttery door and locked it, and told Little John that he would have to make himself happy till his lord returned.

Rude words mattered nothing to Little John, who was not accustomed to be baulked by trifles, so he gave a mighty kick which burst open the door, and then ate and drank as much as he would, and when he had finished all there was in the buttery, he went down into the kitchen.

Now the Sheriff's cook was a strong man and a bold one, and had no mind to let another man play the king in his kitchen; so he gave Little John three smart blows, which were returned heartily. "Thou art a brave man and hardy," said Little John, "and a good fighter withal. I have a sword, take you another, and let us see which is the better man of us twain."

The cook did as he was bid, and for two hours they fought, neither of them harming the other. "Fellow," said Little John at last, "you are one of the best swordsmen that I ever saw—and if you could shoot as well with the bow, I would take you back to the merry greenwood, and Robin Hood would give you twenty marks a year and two changes of clothing."

"Put up your sword," said the cook, "and I will go with you. But first we will have some food in my kitchen, and carry off a little of the gold that is in the Sheriff's treasure house."

They ate and drank till they wanted no more, then they broke the locks of the treasure house, and took of the silver as much as they could carry, three hundred pounds and more, and departed unseen by anyone to Robin in the forest.

# PART VII.

"Welcome! welcome!" cried Robin when he saw them, "welcome, too, to the fair yeoman you bring with you. What tidings from Nottingham, Little John?"

"The proud Sheriff greets you, and sends you by my hand his cook and his silver vessels, and three hundred pounds and three also."

Robin shook his head, for he knew better than to believe Little John's tale. "It was never by his good will that you brought such treasure to me," he answered, and Little John, fearing that he might be ordered to take it back again, slipped away into the forest to carry out a plan that had just come into his head.

He ran straight on for five miles, till he came up with the Sheriff, who was still hunting, and flung himself on his knees before him.

"Reynold Greenleaf," cried the Sheriff, "what are you doing here, and where have you been?"

"I have been in the forest, where I saw a fair hart of a green colour, and sevenscore deer feeding hard by."

"That sight would I see too," said the Sheriff.

"Then follow me," answered Little John, and he ran back the way he came, the Sheriff following on horseback, till they turned a corner of the forest, and found themselves in Robin Hood's presence. "Sir, here is the master-hart," said Little John.

Still stood the proud Sheriff,
A sorry man was he,
"Woe be to you, Reynold Greenleaf,
Thou hast betrayed me!"

"It was not my fault," answered Little John, "but the fault of your servants, master. For they would not give me my dinner," and he went away to see to the supper.

It was spread under the greenwood tree, and they sat down to it, hungry men all. But when the Sheriff saw himself served from his own vessels, his appetite went from him.

PART VII.

# When the Sheriff saw his own vessels his appetite went from him

"Take heart, man," said Robin Hood, "and think not we will poison you. For charity's sake, and for the love of Little John, your life shall be granted you. Only for twelve months you shall dwell with me, and learn what it is to be an outlaw."

To the Sheriff this punishment was worse to bear than the loss of gold or silver dishes, and earnestly he begged Robin Hood to set him free, vowing he would prove himself the best friend that ever the foresters had.

Neither Robin nor any of his men believed him, but he swore that he would never seek to do them harm, and that if he found any of them in evil plight he would deliver them out of it. With that Robin let him go.

# PART VIII.

*HOW ROBIN MET FRIAR TUCK.*

In many ways life in the forest was dull in the winter, and often the days passed slowly; but in summer, when the leaves were green, and flowers and ferns covered all the woodland, Robin Hood and his men would come out of their warm resting places, like the rabbits and the squirrels, and would play too. Races they ran to stretch their legs, or leaping matches were arranged, or they would shoot at a mark. Anything was pleasant when the grass was soft once more under their feet.

"Who can kill a hart of grace five hundred paces off?" So said Robin to his men in the bright May time; and they went into the wood and tried their skill, and in the end it was Little John who brought down the "hart of grace," to the great joy of Robin Hood.

"I would ride my horse a hundred miles to find one who could match with thee," he said to Little John, and Will Scarlett, who was perhaps rather jealous of this mighty deed, answered with a laugh, "There lives a friar in Fountains Abbey who would beat both him and you."

Now Robin Hood did not like to be told that any man could shoot better than himself or his foresters, so he swore lustily that he would neither eat nor drink till he had seen that friar. Leaving his men where they were, he put on a coat of mail and a steel cap, took his shield and sword, slung his bow over his shoulder, and filled his quiver with arrows. Thus armed, he set forth to Fountains Dale.

By the side of the river a friar was walking, armed like Robin, but without a bow. At this sight Robin jumped from his horse, which he tied to a thorn, and called to the friar to carry him over the water or it would cost him his life.

The friar said nothing, but hoisted Robin on his broad back and marched into the river. Not a word was spoken till they reached the other side, when Robin leaped lightly down, and was going on his way when the friar stopped him. "Not so fast, my fine fellow," said he. "It is my turn now, and you shall take me across the river, or woe will betide you."

So Robin carried him, and when they had reached the side from which they had started, he set down the friar and jumped for the second time on his back, and bade him take him whence he had come. The friar strode into the stream with his burden, but as soon as they got to the middle he bent his head and Robin fell into the water. "Now you can sink or swim as you like," said the friar, as he stood and laughed.

# Friar Tuck upsets Robin Hood

Robin Hood swam to a bush of golden broom, and pulled himself out of the water, and while the friar was scrambling out Robin fitted an arrow to his bow and let fly at him. But the friar quickly held up his shield, and the arrow fell harmless.

"Shoot on, my fine fellow, shoot on all day if you like," shouted the friar, and Robin shot till his arrows were gone, but always missed his mark. Then they took their swords, and at four of the afternoon they were still fighting.

By this time Robin's strength was wearing, and he felt he could not fight much more. "A boon, a boon!" cried he. "Let me but blow three blasts on my horn, and I will thank you on my bended knees for it."

The friar told him to blow as many blasts as he liked, and in an instant the forest echoed with his horn; it was but a few minutes before "half a hundred yeomen were racing over the lea". The friar stared when he saw them; then, turning to Robin, he begged of him a boon also, and leave being granted he gave three whistles, which were followed by the noise of a great crashing through the trees, as fifty great dogs bounded towards him.

"Here's a dog for each of your men," said the friar, "and I myself for you"; but the dogs did not listen to his words, for two of them rushed at Robin, and tore his mantle of Lincoln green from off his back. His men were too busy defending themselves to take heed of their master's plight, for every arrow shot at a dog was caught and held in the creature's mouth.

Robin's men were not used to fight with dogs, and felt they were getting beaten. At last Little John bade the friar call off his dogs, and as he did not do so at once he let fly some arrows, which this time left half a dozen dead on the ground.

"Hold, hold, my good fellow," said the friar, "till your master and I can come to a bargain," and when the bargain was made this was how it ran. That the friar was to forswear Fountains Abbey and join Robin Hood, and that he should be paid a golden noble every Sunday throughout the year, besides a change of clothes on each holy day.

This Friar had kept Fountains Dale
Seven long years or more,
There was neither Knight, nor Lord, nor Earl
Could make him yield before.

But now he became one of the most famous members of Robin Hood's men under the name of Friar Tuck.

# PART IX.

*HOW ROBIN HOOD AND LITTLE JOHN FELL OUT.*

One Whitsunday morning, when the sun was shining and the birds singing, Robin Hood called to Little John to come with him into Nottingham to hear Mass. As was their custom, they took their bows, and on the way Little John proposed that they should shoot a match with a penny for a wager.

Robin, who held that he himself shot better than any man living, laughed in scorn, and told Little John that he should have three tries to his master's one, which John without more ado accepted.

But Robin soon repented both of his offer and his scorn, for Little John speedily won five shillings, whereat Robin became angry and smote Little John with his hand.

Little John was not the man to bear being treated so, and he told Robin roundly that he would never more own him for master, and straightway turned back into the wood.

At this Robin was ashamed of what he had done, but his pride would not suffer him to say so, and he continued his way to Nottingham, and entered the Church of St. Mary, not without secret fears, for the Sheriff of the town was ever his enemy. However, there he was and there he meant to stay.

He knelt down before the great cross in the sight of all the people, but none knew him save one monk only, and he stole out of church and ran to the Sheriff, and bade him come quickly and take his foe.

The Sheriff was not slow to do the monk's bidding, and, calling his men to follow him, he marched to the church. The noise they made in entering caused Robin to look round. "Alas, alas," he said to himself, "now miss I Little John."

But he drew his two-handed sword and laid about him in such wise that twelve of the Sheriff's men lay dead before him. Then Robin found himself face to face with the Sheriff, and gave him a fierce blow; but his sword broke on the Sheriff's head, and he had shot away all his arrows. So the men closed round him, and bound his arms.

Ill news travels fast, and not many hours had passed before the foresters heard that their master was in prison. They wept and moaned and wrung their hands, and seemed to have gone suddenly mad, till Little John bade them pluck up their hearts and help him to deal with the monk.

# PART X.

The next morning Little John hid himself, and waited with a comrade, Much by name, till he saw the monk riding along the road, with a page behind him, carrying letters from the Sheriff to the King telling of Robin's capture.

"Whence come you?" asked Little John, going up to the monk, "and can you give us tidings of a false outlaw named Robin Hood, who was taken prisoner yesterday? He robbed both me and my fellow of twenty marks, and glad should we be to hear of his undoing."

"He robbed me, too," said the monk, "of a hundred pounds and more, but I have laid hands on him, and for that you may thank me."

"I thank you so much that, with your leave, I and my friend will bear you company," answered Little John; "for in this forest are many wild men who own Robin Hood for leader, and you ride along this road at the peril of your life."

They went on together, talking the while, when suddenly Little John seized the horse by the head and pulled down the monk by his hood.

"He was my master," said Little John,
"That you have brought to bale,
Never shall you come at the King
For to tell him that tale."

At these words the monk uttered loud cries, but Little John took no heed of him, and smote off his head, as Much had already smitten off that of the page, lest he should carry the news of what had happened back to the Sheriff. After this they buried the bodies, and, taking the letters, carried them themselves to the King.

When they arrived at the Palace, in the presence of the King, Little John fell on his knees and held the letter out. "God save you, my liege lord," he said; and the King unfolded the letters and read them.

"There never was yeoman in Merry England I longed so sore to see," he said. "But where is the monk that should have brought these letters?"

"He died by the way," answered Little John; and the King asked no more questions.

Twenty pounds each he ordered his treasurer to give to Much and to Little John, and made them yeomen of the crown. After which he handed his own seal to Little John and ordered him to bear it to the Sheriff, and bid him without delay bring Robin Hood unhurt into his presence.

Little John did as the King bade him, and the Sheriff, at sight of the seal, gave him and Much welcome, and set a feast before them, at which John led him to drink heavily. Soon he fell asleep, and then the two outlaws stole softly to the prison. Here John ran the porter through the body for trying to stop his entrance, and, taking the keys, hunted through the cells until he had found Robin. Thrusting a sword into his hand Little John whispered to his master to follow him, and they crept along till they reached the lowest part of the city wall, from which they jumped and were safe and free.

"Now, farewell," said Little John, "I have done you a good turn for an ill." "Not so," answered Robin Hood, "I make you master of my men and me," but Little John would hear nothing of it. "I only wish to be your comrade, and thus it shall be," he replied.

"Little John has beguiled us both," said the King, when he heard of the adventure.

# PART XI.

*HOW THE KING VISITED ROBIN HOOD.*

Now the King had no mind that Robin Hood should do as he willed, and called his Knights to follow him to Nottingham, where they would lay plans how best to take captive the felon. Here they heard sad tales of Robin's misdoings, and how of the many herds of wild deer that had been wont to roam the forest in some places scarce one remained. This was the work of Robin Hood and his merry men, on whom the King swore vengeance with a great oath.

"I would I had this Robin Hood in my hands," cried he, "and an end should soon be put to his doings." So spake the King; but an old Knight, full of days and wisdom, answered him and warned him that the task of taking Robin Hood would be a sore one, and best let alone.

The King, who had seen the vanity of his hot words the moment that he had uttered them, listened to the old man, and resolved to bide his time, if perchance some day Robin should fall into his power.

All this time, and for six weeks later that he dwelt in Nottingham, the King could hear nothing of Robin, who seemed to have vanished into the earth with his merry men, though one by one the deer were vanishing too!

At last one day a forester came to the King, and told him that if he would see Robin he must come with him and take five of his best Knights. The King eagerly sprang up to do his bidding, and the six men clad in monks' clothes mounted their palfreys and rode down to the Abbey, the King wearing an Abbot's broad hat over his crown, and singing as he passed through the green wood.

Suddenly at the turn of a path Robin and his archers appeared before them.

"By your leave, Sir Abbot," said Robin, seizing the King's bridle, "you will stay a while with us. Know that we are yeomen, who live upon the King's deer, and other food have we none. Now you have abbeys and churches, and gold in plenty; therefore give us some of it, in the name of holy charity."

"I have no more than forty pounds with me," answered the King, "but sorry I am it is not a hundred, for you should have had it all."

So Robin took the forty pounds, and gave half to his men, and then told the King he might go on his way. "I thank you," said the King, "but I would have you know that our liege lord has bid me bear you his seal, and pray you to come to Nottingham."

At this message Robin bent his knee.

"I love no man in all the world

So well as I do my King";

he cried, "and Sir Abbot, for thy tidings, which fill my heart with joy, to-day thou shalt dine with me, for love of my King". Then he led the King into an open place, and Robin took a horn and blew it loud, and at its blast seven score of young men came speedily to do his will.

"They are quicker to do his bidding than my men are to do mine," said the King to himself.

Speedily the foresters set out the dinner, venison, and white bread, and the good red wine, and Robin and Little John served the King. "Make good cheer," said Robin, "Abbot, for charity, and then you shall see what sort of life we lead, that so you may tell our King."

When he had finished eating, the archers took their bows, and hung rose-garlands up with a string, and every man was to shoot through the garland. If he failed, he should have a buffet on the head from Robin.

Good bowmen as they were, few managed to stand the test. Little John and Will Scarlett, and Much, all shot wide of the mark, and at length no one was left in but Robin himself and Gilbert of the Wide Hand. Then Robin fired his last bolt, and it fell three fingers from the garland. "Master," said Gilbert, "you have lost, stand forth and take your punishment."

"I will take it," answered Robin, "but, Sir Abbot, I pray you that I may suffer it at your hands."

The King hesitated. "It did not become him," he said, "to smite such a stout yeoman," but Robin bade him smite on; so he turned up his sleeve, and gave Robin such a buffet on the head that he rolled upon the ground.

"There is pith in your arm," said Robin. "Come, shoot a main with me." And the King took up a bow, and in so doing his hat fell back and Robin saw his face.

# PART XI.

# There is pith in your arm said Robin Hood

"My lord the King of England, now I know you well," cried he, and he fell on his knees and all the outlaws with him. "Mercy I ask, my lord the King, for my men and me."

"Mercy I grant," then said the King, "and therefore I came hither, to bid you and your men leave the greenwood and dwell in my Court with me."

"So shall it be," answered Robin, "I and my men will come to your Court, and see how your service liketh us."

# PART XII.

*ROBIN AT COURT.*

"Have you any green cloth," asked the King, "that you could sell to me?" and Robin brought out thirty yards and more, and clad the King and his men in coats of Lincoln green. "Now we will all ride to Nottingham," said he, and they went merrily, shooting by the way.

The people of Nottingham saw them coming, and trembled as they watched the dark mass of Lincoln green drawing near over the fields. "I fear lest our King be slain," whispered one to another, "and if Robin Hood gets into the town there is not one of us whose life is safe"; and every man, woman, and child made ready to fly.

The King laughed out when he saw their fright, and called them back. Right glad were they to hear his voice, and they feasted and made merry. A few days later the King returned to London, and Robin dwelt in his Court for twelve months. By that time he had spent a hundred pounds, for he gave largely to the Knights and Squires he met, and great renown he had for his open-handedness.

But his men, who had been born under the shadow of the forest, could not live amid streets and houses. One by one they slipped away, till only Little John and Will Scarlett were left. Then Robin himself grew home-sick, and at the sight of some young men shooting, he thought upon the time when he was accounted the best archer in all England, and went straightway to the King and begged for leave to go on a pilgrimage to Bernisdale.

"I may not say you nay," answered the King, "seven nights you may be gone and no more." And Robin thanked him, and that evening set out for the greenwood.

It was early morning when he reached it at last, and listened thirstily to the notes of singing birds, great and small.

"It seems long since I was here," he said to himself; "it would give me great joy if I could bring down a deer once more;" and he shot a great hart, and blew his horn, and all the outlaws of the forest came flocking round him.

"Welcome," they said, "our dear master, back to the greenwood tree," and they threw off their caps and fell on their knees before him in delight at his return.

# PART XIII.

*THE DEATH OF ROBIN HOOD.*

For two and twenty years Robin Hood dwelt in Sherwood Forest after he had run away from Court, and naught that the King could say would tempt him back again. At the end of that time he fell ill; he neither ate nor drank, and had no care for the things he loved, "I must go to merry Kirkley," said he, "and have my blood let."

But Will Scarlett, who heard his words, spoke roundly to him. "Not by my leave, nor without a hundred bowmen at your back. For there abides an evil man, who is sure to quarrel with you, and you will need us badly."

"If you are afraid, Will Scarlett, you may stay at home, for me," said Robin, "and in truth no man will I take with me, save Little John only, to carry my bow."

"Bear your bow yourself, master, and I will bear mine, and we will shoot for a penny as we ride."

"Very well, let it be so," said Robin, and they went on merrily enough till they came to some women weeping sorely near a stream.

"What is the matter, good wives?" said Robin Hood.

"We weep for Robin Hood and his dear body, which to-day must let blood," was their answer.

"Pray why do you weep for me?" asked Robin; "the Prioress is the daughter of my aunt, and my cousin, and well I know she would not do me harm for all the world."

And he passed on, with Little John at his side.

Soon they reached the Priory, where they were let in by the Prioress herself, who bade them welcome heartily, and not the less because Robin handed her twenty pounds in gold as payment for his stay, and told her if he cost her more she was to let him know of it.

Then she began to bleed him, and for long Robin said nothing, giving her credit for kindness and for knowing her art, but at length so much blood came from him that he suspected treason.

He tried to open the door, for she had left him alone in the room, but it was locked fast, and while the blood was still flowing he could not escape from the casement. So he lay down for many hours, and none came near him, and at length the blood stopped.

Slowly Robin uprose and staggered to the lattice-window, and blew thrice on his horn; but the blast was so low, and so little like what Robin was wont to give, that Little John, who was watching for some sound, felt that his master must be nigh to death.

At this thought he started to his feet, and ran swiftly to the Priory. He broke the locks of all the doors that stood between him and Robin Hood, and soon entered the chamber where his master lay, white, with nigh all his blood gone from him.

"I crave a boon of you, dear master," cried Little John.

"And what is that boon," said Robin Hood, "which Little John begs of me?" And Little John answered, "It is to burn fair Kirkley Hall, and all the nunnery."

ROBIN HOOD SHOOTS HIS LAST ARROW

# Robin Hood shoots his last arrow

But Robin Hood, in spite of the wrong that had been done him, would not listen to Little John's cry for revenge. "I never hurt a woman in all my life," he said, "nor a man that was in her company. But now my time is done, that know I well; so give me my bow and a broad arrow, and wheresoever it falls there shall my grave be digged. Lay a green sod under my head and another at my feet, and put beside me my bow, which ever made sweetest music to my ears, and see that green and gravel make my grave. And, Little John, take care that I have length enough and breadth enough to lie in." So he loosened his last arrow from the string and then died, and where the arrow fell Robin was buried.

# WAYLAND THE SMITH.

# PART I.

Right up to the north of Norway and Sweden, looking straight at the Pole, lies the country of Finmark. It is very cold and very bare, and for half the year very dark; but inside its stony mountains are rich stores of metals, and the strong, ugly men of the country spent their lives in digging out the ore and in working it.

Like many people who dwell in mountains, they saw and heard strange things, which were unknown to the inhabitants of the lands to the south.

Now in Finmark there were three brothers whose names were Slagfid, Eigil, and Wayland, all much handsomer and cleverer than their neighbours. They had some money of their own, but this did not prevent them working as hard as anyone else; and as they were either very clever or very lucky, they were soon in a fair way to grow rich.

One day they went to a new part of the mountains which was yet untouched, and began to throw up the earth with their pick-axes; but instead of the iron they expected to see, they found they had lighted upon a mine of gold.

This discovery pleased them greatly and their blows became stronger and harder, for the gold was deep in the rock and it was not easy to get it out.

At last a huge lump rolled out at their feet, and when they picked it up they saw three stones shining in it, one red and one blue and one green. They took it home to their mother, who began to weep bitterly at the sight of it. "What is the matter?" asked her sons anxiously, for they knew things lay open to her which were hidden from others.

"Ah, my sons," she said as soon as she could speak, "you will have much happiness, but I shall be forced to part with you. Therefore I shed tears, for I hoped that only death would divide us! Green is the grass, blue is the sky, red are the roses, golden is the maiden. The Noras" (for so in that country they called the Fates) "beckon you to a land where green fields lie under a blue sky, fields where golden-haired maidens lie among the flowers."

Great was the joy of the three brothers when they heard the words of their mother; for they hated the looks of the women who dwelt about them, and longed to see the maidens of the south. Next morning they rose early and buckled on their swords and coats of mail, and fastened on their heads helmets that they had made the day before from the lump of gold. In the centre of Slagfid's helmet was the green stone, and in the centre of Eigil's was the blue stone, and in the centre of Wayland's was the red stone; and when they were ready they put their reindeers into their sledges, and set out over the snow.

# PART II.

When they reached the mountains where only yesterday they had been digging, they saw by the light of the moon a host of little men running to meet them. They were dressed all in grey, except for their caps, which were red; they had red eyes, too, and black tongues, which never ceased chattering.

These were the mountain elves, and when they came near they formed themselves into a fairy ring, and sang while they danced round it;—

Will you leave us? Will you leave us?
Slagfid, Eigil, and Wayland, sons of a King.
Is not the emerald better than grass?
Is not the ruby better than roses?
Is not the sapphire better than the sky?
Why do you leave the mountains of Finmark?

But Eigil was impatient and struck his reindeer, that willing beast which flies like the wind and needs not the touch of a whip. It bounded forward in surprise, and knocked down one of the elves that stood in its path. But the hands of his brothers laid hold of the reins, and stopped the reindeer, and sang again:—

The Finlander's world, the Finlander's joy
Lies under the earth;
Seek not without what we offer within,
Despise not the elves small and dark though they be.
The best is within, do not seek it without.
The Finlander's world, the Finlander's joy,
Lies under the earth.

Slagfid struck his reindeer. It bounded forward and struck down an elf who stood in its road. Then his brothers stood in its path, and stopped the reindeer, and sang:—

Because Slagfid struck his reindeer,
Because Eigil struck his reindeer,
Our hatred shall follow you.
A time of weal, a time of woe, a time of grief, a time of joy.
Because Wayland also forsook us,
Though he struck not the reindeer,

A time of weal, a time of woe, a time of grief, a time of joy.

Farewell, O Finlanders, sons of a King.

Their voices died away as they crossed a bright strip of moonlight, which lay between them and the mountains and so they were seen no more.

The brothers thought no more about them or their words, but went swiftly on their way south, sleeping at night in their reindeer skins.

After many days they came to a lake full of fish, in a place which was called the Valley of Wolves, because of the number of wolves which hid there. But the Finlanders did not mind the wolves, and built a house close to the lake, and hunted bears, and caught fish through holes in the ice, till winter had passed away and spring had come. Then one day they noticed that the sky was blue and the earth covered with flowers.

By-and-by they noticed something more, and that was that three maidens were sitting on the grass, spinning flax on the bank of a stream. Their eyes were blue, and their skins were white as the snow on the mountains, while instead of the mantles of swansdown they generally wore, golden hair covered their shoulders.

The hearts of the brothers beat as they looked on the maidens, who were such as they had often dreamed of, but had never seen; and as they drew near they found to their surprise that the maidens were dressed each in red, green, and blue garments, and the meadow was so thickly dotted with yellow flowers that it seemed as if it were a mass of solid gold.

PART II.

*The Three Women By The Stream*

# The three women by the stream

"Hail, noble princes! Hail, Slagfid, Eigil, and Wayland," sang the maidens.
"Swanvite, Alvilda, and Alruna are sent by the Norns,
To bring joy to the princes of Finmark"
Then the tongues of the young men were unloosed, and Slagfid married Swanvite, Eigil Alruna, and Wayland Alvilda.

# PART III.

For nine years they all lived on the shores of the lake, and no people in the world were as happy as these six; till one morning the three wives stood before their husbands and said with weeping eyes:—

"Dear lords, the time has now come when we must bid you farewell, for we are not allowed to stay with you any longer.. We are Norns—or, as some call us, Valkyrie. Nine years of joy are granted to us, but these are paid for by nine years during which we hover round the combatants on every field of battle. But bear your souls in patience, for on earth all things have an end, and in nine years we will return to be your wives as before."

"But we shall begetting old then," answered the brothers, "and you will have forgotten us. Stay now, we pray you, for we love you well."

"*We* are not mortals to grow old," said the Norns, "and true love does not grow old either. Still, we do not wish you to fall sick with grieving, so we leave you these three keys, with which you may open the mountain, and busy yourselves by digging out the treasures it contains. By the time the nine years are over you will have become rich and men of renown." So they laid down the keys and vanished.

For a long while the young men only left their houses to seek for food, so dreary had the Valley of Wolves become. At last Slagfid and Eigil could bear it no longer, and declared they would travel through the whole world till they found their wives; but Wayland, the youngest, determined to stay at home.

"You would do much better to remain where you are," said he. "You do not know in which direction to look for them, and it is useless to seek on earth for those who fly through the air. You will only lose yourselves, and starve, and when the nine years are ended who can tell where you may be?"

But his words fell on deaf ears; for Slagfid and Eigil merely filled their wallets with food and their horns with drink, and prepared to take leave of their brother. Wayland embraced them weeping, for he feared that he should never more see them, and once again he implored them to give up their quest. Slagfid and Eigil only shook their heads. "We have no rest, night or day, without them," they said, and they begged him to look after their property till they came back again.

Wayland saw that more words would be wasted, so he walked with them to the edge of the forest, where their ways would part. Then Slagfid said: "Our fathers, when they went a journey, left behind them a token by which it might be known whether they were dead or alive, and I will do so also." So he stamped heavily on the soft ground, and added, "As long as this footmark remains sharp and clear, I shall be safe. If it is filled with water I shall be drowned; if with blood, I shall have fallen in battle. But if it is filled with earth an illness will have killed me, and I shall lie under the ground." Thus he did, and Eigil did likewise. Then they cut stout sticks to aid their journeys, and went their ways. Wayland stood gazing after them as long as they were in sight, and then he went sadly home.

# PART IV.

Slagfid and Eigil walked steadily on through the day, and when evening came they reached a stream bordered with trees, where they took off their golden helmets and sat down to rest and eat. They had gone far that day and were tired, and drank somewhat heavily, so that they knew not what they did. "If I lose my Swanvite," said Slagfid, "I am undone. She is the fairest woman that sun ever looked on, or that man ever loved."

"It is a lie," answered Eigil. "I know one lovelier still, and her name is Alruna. Odin does not love Freya so fondly as Eigil adores her."

"It is no lie," cried Slagfid, "and may shame fall on him who slanders me."

"And I," answered Eigil, "stand to what I have said, and declare that you are the liar." At this they both drew their swords and fell fighting, till Slagfid struck Eigil's helmet so hard that the jewel flew into a thousand pieces, while Eigil himself fell backwards into the river.

Slagfid stood still, leaning on his sword and looking at the river into which his brother had fallen. Suddenly the trees behind him rustled, and a voice came out of them, saying, "A time of weal, a time of woe, a time of tears, a time of death"; and though he could see nothing he remembered the mountain elves, and thought how true their prophecy had been. "I have slain my brother," he said to himself, "my wife has forsaken me; I am miserable and alone. What shall I do? Go back to Wayland, or follow Eigil into the river? No. After all I may find my wife. The Norns do not always bring misfortune."

As he spoke a light gleamed in the darkness of the night, and, looking up, Slagfid saw it was shed by a bright star which seemed to be drawing nearer, and the nearer it drew its shape seemed to change into a human figure. Then Slagfid knew that it was his wife, Swanvite, floating just over his head and encircled by a rim of clear green light.

He could not speak for joy, but held out his arms to her. She beckoned to him to follow her, and Slagfid, flinging away his sword and coat of mail, began to climb the mountain.

Half way up it seemed to him as if a hand from behind was pulling him back, and turning he fancied he beheld his mother and heard her say: "My son, seek not after vain shadows, which yet may be your ruin."

The words caused Slagfid to pause for a moment. Then the figure of Swanvite danced before him and beckoned to him again, and his mother was forgotten. There were rivers to swim, precipices to climb, chasms to leap, but he passed them all gladly, till at last he noticed that the higher he got the less the figure seemed like Swanvite.

He felt frightened and tried to turn back, but he could not. On he had to go, till just as he reached the top of the mountain the first rays of the sun appeared above the horizon, and he saw that, instead of Swanvite, he had followed a black elf.

He paused and looked over the green plain that lay thousands of feet below him, cool and inviting after the stony mountain up which he had come. "A time of death," whispered the black elf in his ear, and Slagfid flung himself over the precipice.

# PART V.

After his brothers had forsaken him Wayland went to bed lonely and sad; but the next morning he got up and looked at the three keys that the Noras had left behind them. One was of copper, one was of iron, and one was of gold.

Taking up the copper one, he walked to the mountain till he reached a flat wall of rock. He laid his key against it, and immediately the mountain flew open and showed a cave where everything was green. Green emeralds studded the rocks, green crystals hung from the ceiling or formed rows of pillars, even the copper which made the walls of the cave had a coating of green. Wayland broke off a huge projecting lump and left the cave, which instantly closed up so that not a crack remained to tell where the opening had been.

He carried the lump home, and put it into the fire till all the earth and stones which clung to it were burned away; and then he fashioned the pure copper into a helmet, and in the front of the helmet he set three of his largest emeralds.

This occupied some days, and when it was done he took the iron key, and went to another mountain, and laid the key against the rock, which flew open like the other one. But now the walls were of iron, which shone like blue steel, while sapphires glittered in the midst.

Wayland gazed with wonder at all these things; then he broke off a piece of the iron, and carried it home with him.

For many days after he busied himself in forging a sword that was so supple he could wind it round his body, and so sharp it could cut through a rock as if it had been a stick. In the handle and in the sheath he set some of the finest sapphires that he had brought away with him.

When all was finished he laid the sword aside, and returned to the mountain, with the golden key. This time the mountain parted, and he saw before him an archway, with a glimpse of the sea in the distance.

Before the entrance roses were lying, and inside the golden walls sparkled with rubies, while branches of red coral filled every crevice. Vines climbed around the pillars, and bore large bunches of red grapes.

Wayland stood long, looking at these marvels; then he plucked some of the grapes, broke off a lump of gold, and set out home again.

Next day he began to make himself a golden breastplate, and in it he placed the jewels, and it was so bright that you could have seen the glitter a mile off.

After he had tried all the three keys, and found out the secrets of the mountain, Wayland felt dull. So his mind went back to his brothers, and he wondered how they had fared all this time.

The first thing he did was to go to the edge of the forest, and see if he could find the two footprints they had left.

He soon arrived at the spot where they had taken farewell of each other, but a blue pool of water covered the trace of Eigil's foot. He turned to look at the impression made by Slagfid, but on that fresh green grass had sprung up over it, and on a birch-tree near it a bird had perched, which sang a mournful song.

Then Wayland knew that his brothers were dead, and he returned to his hut, grieving sore.

# PART VI.

It was a long time before Wayland could bring himself to go out, so great was his sorrow; but at last he roused himself from his misery, and went to the mountain for more gold, meaning to work hard till the nine years should be over and he should get his wife back again.

All day long he stood in his forge, smelting and hammering, till he had made hundreds of suits of armour and thousands of swords, and his fame travelled far, so that all men spoke of his industry.

At last he grew tired of making armour, and hammered a number of gold rings, which he strung on strips of bark, and as he hammered he thought of Alvilda his wife, and how the rings would gleam on her arms when once she came back again.

Now at this time Nidud the Little reigned over Sweden, and was hated by his people, for he was vain and cowardly and had many other bad qualities. It came to his ears that away in the forests lived a man who was very rich, and worked all day long in pure gold.

The King was one of those people who could not bear to see anyone with things which he did not himself possess, and he began to make plans how to get hold of Wayland's wealth.

At length he called together his chief counsellors, and said to them: "I hear a man has come to my kingdom who is called Wayland, famous in many lands for his skill in sword-making. I have set men to inquire after him, and I have found that when first he came here he was poor and of no account, so he must have grown rich either by magic or else by violence. I command, therefore, that my stoutest men-at-arms should buckle on their iron breastplates and ride in the dead of night to Wayland's house, and seize his goods and his person."

"King Nidud," answered one of the courtiers, "that you should take himself and his goods is well, but why send a troop of soldiers against one man? If he is no sorcerer, then a single one of your soldiers could take him captive; but if, on the other hand, he is a magician, then a whole army could do nothing with him against his will."

At this reply the King flew in a rage, and, snatching up a sword, ran it through his counsellor's body; then, turning to the rest, told them that they would suffer the same fate if they refused to submit to his will.

So the men-at-arms put on all their armour, and, mounting their horses, set forth at sunset to Wayland's house, King Nidud riding at their head. The door stood wide open, and they entered quietly, in deadly fear lest Wayland should attack them.

But no one was inside, and they looked about, their eyes dazzled by the gold on the walls. The King gazed with wonder and delight at the long string of golden rings, and, slipping the finest off a strip of bark, placed it on his finger.

At that moment steps were heard in the outer court, and the King hastily desired his followers to hide themselves, and not to stir till he signed to them to do so.

In another moment Wayland stood in the doorway, carrying on his shoulders a bear which he had killed with his spear and was bringing home for supper.

He was both tired and hungry, for he had been hunting all day; but he had first to skin the animal, and make a bright fire, before he could cut off some steaks and cook them at the end of the spear. Then he poured some mead into a cup and drank, as he always did, to the memory of his brothers. After that he spread out his bear's skin to dry in the wind, and this done he stretched himself out on his bed and went to sleep.

# PART VII.

King Nidud waited till he thought all was safe, then crept forth with his men, who held heavy chains in their hands wherewith to chain the sleeping Wayland. But the task was harder than they expected, for he started up in wrath, asking why he should be treated so. "If you want my gold, take it and release me. It is useless fighting against such odds."

"I am no robber," said Nidud, "but I am your King."

"You do me much honour," replied Wayland, "but what have I done to be loaded with chains like this?"

"Wayland, I know you well," said Nidud. "Poor enough you were when you came from Finmark, and now your jewels are finer and your drinking cups heavier than mine."

"If I am indeed a thief," answered Wayland, "then you do well to load me with chains and lead me bound into your dungeons; but if not, I ask again, Why do you misuse me?"

"Riches do not come of themselves," said Nidud, "and if you are not a thief, then you must be a magician and must be watched."

"If I were a magician," answered Wayland, "it would be easy for me to burst these bonds. I know not that I have ever wronged any man, but if he can prove it, I will restore it to him tenfold. As to the gifts that may come from the gods, no man should grudge them to his fellow. Therefore release me, O King, and I will pay whatever ransom you may fix."

But Nidud only bade his guards take him away, and Wayland, seeing that resistance availed nothing, went with them quietly.

By the King's orders he was thrown into a dark hole fifteen fathoms under ground, and the soldiers then came and robbed the house of all its treasures, which they took to the Palace. The ring which Wayland had made for Alvilda, Nidud gave to his daughter, Banvilda.

One day the Queen was in her own room, when the King came in to ask her advice as to how best to deal with Wayland, as he did not think it wise to put him to death, for he hoped to make some profit out of his skill. "His heart will beat high," said the Queen, "when he sees his good sword, and beholds his ring on Banvilda's finger. But cut asunder the sinews of his strength, so that he can never more escape from us, and keep him a prisoner."

The King was pleased with the Queen's words, and sent soldiers to carry Wayland to a tower on an island. The sinews of his legs were cut so that he could not swim away; but they gave him his boots, and the chests of gold they had found in his house. Here he was left, with nothing to do from morning till night, but to make helmets and drinking cups and splendid armour for the King.

# PART VIII.

On this island Wayland remained for a whole year, chained to a stone and visited by no one but the King, who came from time to time to see how his prisoner was getting on with a suit of golden armour he had been ordered to make.

The shield was also of gold, and on it Wayland had beaten out a history of the gods and their great deeds. He was very miserable, for the hope of revenge which had kept him alive seemed as far off as ever in its fulfilment, and finding a sword he had lately forged lying close to his hand, he seized it, with the intent of putting an end to his wretched life.

He had hardly stretched out his hand, when a bird began to sing at the iron bars of his window, while the evening sun shone into his prison. "I should like to see the world once more," thought he, and, raising himself on the stone to which his chain was fastened, he was able to look at what lay beneath him.

The sea washed the base of the rock on which the tower was built, and on a neck of land a little way off some children were playing before the door of a hut. Everything was bathed in red light from the glow of the setting sun.

Wayland stood quite still on top of the stone, gazing at the scene with all his eyes, yet thinking of the land of his birth, which was so different. Then he looked again at the sea, which was already turning to steel, and in the distance he saw something moving on the waves.

As it came nearer he discovered it was a water sprite, singing a song which blended with the murmur of the waves and the notes of the bird. And the song put new life and courage into his heart, for it told him that if he would endure and await the pleasure of the gods, joy would be his one day.

The sprite finished her song, and smiled up at Wayland at the window before turning and swimming over the waves till she dived beneath them. That same instant the bird flew away, and the moon was covered by a cloud. But Wayland's heart was cheered, and when he lay down to rest he slept quietly.

Some days later the King paid another visit, and suddenly espied the three keys which had been hidden in a corner with some of Wayland's tools.

He at once asked Wayland what they were, and when he would not tell him the King grew so angry that, seizing an axe, he declared that he would put his prisoner to death unless he confessed all he knew. There was no help for it, and Wayland had to say how he came by them and what wonders they wrought. The King heard him with delight and went away, taking the keys with him.

# PART IX.

No time was lost in preparing for a journey to the mountains, and when the King reached the spot described by Wayland he divided his followers into three parties, sending two to await him some distance off, and keeping the third to enter the mountain with himself, if the copper key did the wonders it had done before.

So he gave it to one of the bravest of his men, and told him to lay it against the side of the mountain. The man obeyed, and instantly the mountain split from top to bottom.

The King bade them enter, never doubting that rich spoils awaited him; but instead, the men sank into a green marsh, which swallowed up many of them, while the rest were stung to death by the green serpents hanging from the roof. Those who, like the King, were near the entrance alone escaped.

As soon as he had recovered from the terror into which this adventure had thrown him, he commanded that it should be kept very secret from the other two parties, and desired Storbiorn his Chamberlain, to take the key of iron and the key of gold and deliver them to the leaders of the divisions he had left behind, with orders to try their fortune in different parts of the mountain.

"Give the keys to me, my lord King," answered Storbiorn, "and I shall know what to do with them. These magicians may do their worst, my heart will not beat one whit the faster; and I shall see all that happens."

So he went and gave his message to the two divisions, and one stayed behind while Storbiorn went to the mountain with the other.

When they arrived, the man who held the key laid it against the rock, which burst asunder, and half the men entered at Storbiorn's command.

Suddenly an icy blue stream poured upon them from the depths of the cavern, and drowned most of them before they had time to fly. Only those behind escaped, and Storbiorn bade them go instantly to the King and tell him what had happened.

Then he went to the third troop and marched with them to the rock, where he gave the golden key to one of the men, and ordered him to try it.

The rock flew open at once, and Storbiorn told the men to enter, taking care, however, to keep behind himself. They obeyed and found themselves in a lovely golden cave, whose walls were lit up by thousands of precious stones of every hue.

There was neither sight nor sound to frighten them, and even Storbiorn, when he saw the gold, forgot his prudence and his fears, and followed them in.

In a moment a red fire burst out with a terrific noise, and clouds of smoke poured over them, so that they fell down choked into the flames. Only one man escaped, and he ran back as fast as he could to the King to tell him of the fate of his army.

# PART X.

All this time Wayland was working quietly in his island prison, waiting for the day of his revenge. The suit of golden armour which the King had commanded kept him busy day and night, and, besides the wonderful shield with figures of the gods, he had wrought a coat of mail, a helmet, and armour for the thighs, such as never had been seen before.

The King had invited all his great nobles to meet him at the Palace, when he returned from the mountain, so that they might see his wonderful armour and all the precious things he should bring with him from the caverns.

When Nidud reached his Palace the Queen and Banvilda, their daughter, came forth to meet him, and told him that the great hall was already full of guests, expecting to see the wonders he had brought.

The King said little about his adventures, but went into the armoury to put on his armour in order to appear before his nobles. Piece by piece he fastened it, but he found the helmet so heavy that he could hardly bear it on his head. However, he did not look properly dressed without it, so he had to wear it, though it felt as if a whole mountain was pressing on his forehead. Then, buckling on the sword which Wayland had forged, he entered the hall, and seated himself on the throne.

The Earls were struck dumb by his splendour, and thought at first that it was a god, till they looked under the helmet and saw the ugly little man with the pale cowardly face. So they turned their eyes gladly on the Queen and Princess, both tall and beautiful and glittering with jewels, though inwardly they were not much better than the King.

A magnificent dinner made the nobles feel more at ease, and they begged the King to tell them what man was so skilled in smith's work. Now Nidud had drunk deeply, and longed to revenge himself on Wayland, whom he held to have caused the loss of his army; so he gave the key of the tower to one of his Earls, and bade him take two men and bring forth Wayland, adding that if the next time he visited the tower he should find a grain of gold missing, they should pay for it with their lives.

The three men got a boat, and rowed towards the tower, but on the way one who, like the King, had drunk too much fell into the sea and was drowned. The other two reached the tower in safety, and finding Wayland, blackened with dust, busy at his forge, bade him come just as he was to the boat.

With his hands bound they led him before the King, and said, "We have done your desire, Sir King, and must now hasten back to look for Grullorm, who fell into the sea".

"Leave him where he is," replied Nidud; "and in token of your obedience to my orders I will give you each these golden chains."

The guests had not thought to see the man who had made such wonderful armour helpless and a cripple, and said so to the King. "He was once handsome and stately enough," answered Nidud, "but I have bowed his stubborn head." And the Queen and her daughter laughed and said, "The maidens of Finmark will hardly fancy a lover who cannot stand upright".

WAYLAND MOCKED BY THE QUEEN AND BANVILDA

# Wayland mocked by the Queen and Banvilda

But Wayland stood as if he heard nothing, till the King's son snatched a bone from the table and threw it at his head. Then his patience gave way, and, seizing the bone, he beat Nidud about the head with it till the helmet itself fell off.

The guests all took his side, and said that, though a cripple, he was braver than many men whose legs were straight, and begged the King to allow him to go back to his prison without being teased further.

But the King cried that Wayland had done mischief enough, and must now be punished, and told them the story of his visit to the mountain and the loss of his followers. "It would be a small punishment to put him to death," he said, "for to so wretched a cripple death would be welcome. He may use the gold that is left, but henceforth he shall only have one eye to work with," and the Princess came forward and carried out the cruel sentence herself. Wayland bore it all, saying nothing, but praying the gods to grant him vengeance.

# PART XI.

One night Wayland sat filled with grief and despair, looking out over the sea, when he caught sight of two red lights, bobbing in his direction. He watched them curiously till they vanished beneath the tower.

Soon the key of the door turned, and two men, whom he knew to be the King's sons, talked softly together. He kept very still, and heard one say: "Let us first get as much from the chest as we can carry, then we will put him to death, lest he should betray us to our father."

Then Wayland took a large sword which lay by his side and hid it behind him, and he had scarcely done so when the princes entered the prison. "Greeting to you," said they. "Nidud our father has gone into the country, and as he is so greedy of wealth that he will give us none, we have come here to get it for ourselves. Hand us the key and swear not to tell our father, or you shall die."

"My good lords," answered Wayland, "your request is reasonable, and I am not so foolish as to refuse it. Here is the key, and I will swear not to betray you."

The brothers took the key, and opened the chest, which was still half full of gold. It dazzled their eyes, and they both stooped down so as to see it better. This was what Wayland had waited for, and, seizing his sword, he cut off their heads, which fell into the chest. He then dug a grave for the bodies in the floor of his dungeon. Afterwards he dried the skulls, and made them into two drinking cups wrought with gold. The eyes he set with precious stones, while the teeth he filed till they were shaped like pearls, and strung like a necklace.

As soon as the King came back from his journey he paid a visit to Wayland, who produced the drinking cups which he said were made of some curious shells washed up in a gale.

After some days had passed, some sailors found the princes' boat, which had drifted into the open sea. Their bodies, of course, were not to be found, and the King ordered a splendid funeral feast to be prepared.

On this occasion the new drinking cups were filled with mead, and, besides her necklace, Banvilda wore the ring which her father had taken long ago from Wayland's house.

As was the custom, the feast lasted long, and the guests drank deeply and grew merry. But at midnight their gaiety suddenly came to an end. The King was drinking from the cup of mead, when he felt a violent pain in his head and let the vessel fall. The hues of the armlets that the Queen wore became so strange and dreadful that her eyes suffered agony from looking at em, and she tore them from her arms; while Banvilda was seized with such severe toothache that she could sit at table no longer. The guests at once took leave, but it was not till the sun rose that the pains of their hosts went away.

# PART XII.

In the torture of toothache which she had endured during the night, Banvilda had dashed her arm against the wall, and had broken some of the ornaments off the ring.

She feared to tell her father, who would be sure to punish her, and was in despair how to get the ring mended, when she caught sight of the island on which Wayland's tower stood. "If I had not mocked at him he might have helped me now," thought she.

No other way seemed to offer itself, and in the evening she loosened a boat and began to row to the tower. On the way she met an old merman with a long beard, floating on the waves who warned her not to go on; but she paid no heed, and only rowed the faster.

*The Merman warns Banvilda in vain.*

# The merman warns Banvilda in vain

She entered the tower by a false key, and, holding the ring out to Wayland, begged him to mend it as fast as possible, so that she might return before she was missed. Wayland answered her with courtesy, and promised to do his best, but said that she would have to blow the bellows to keep the forge fire alight. "How comes it that these bellows are sprinkled with blood?" asked Banvilda.

"It is the blood of two young sea dogs," answered Wayland; "they troubled me for long, but I caught them when they least expected it. But blow the bellows harder, I pray you, or I shall never be finished."

Banvilda did as she was told, but soon grew tired and thirsty, and begged Wayland to give her something to drink. He mixed something sweet in a cup, which she swallowed hastily, and soon fell fast asleep on a bench. Then Wayland bound her hands, and placed her in the boat, after which he cut the rope that held it and let it drift out to sea.

This done, he shut the door of the tower, and, taking a piece of gold, he engraved on it the history of all that had happened, and put it where it must meet the King's eye when next he came. "Now is my hour come," he cried with joy, snatching his spear from the wall, but before he could throw himself on it he heard a distant song and the notes of a lute.

By this time the sun was high in the heavens, yet its brightness did not hinder Wayland from seeing a large star, which was floating towards him, and a brilliant rainbow spanned the sky. The flowers on the island unfolded themselves as the star drew near, and he could smell the smell of the roses on the shore.

And now Wayland saw it was no star, but the golden chariot of Freya the goddess, whose blue mantle floated behind her till it was lost in the blue of the sky. On her left was a maiden dressed in garlands of fresh green leaves, and on her right was one clad in a garment of red.

The merman warns Banvilda in vain

· THE CHARIOT OF FREYA ·

# The Chariot of Freya

At the sight Wayland's heart beat high, for he thought of the lump of gold set with jewels, which he and his brothers had found in the mountain so long ago. Fairies fluttered round them, mermaids rose from the depths of the sea to welcome them, and as Freya and her maidens entered the prison Wayland saw that she who wore the red garment was indeed Alvilda. "Wayland," said the goddess, "your time of woe is past. You have suffered much and have avenged your wrongs, and now Odin has granted my prayer that Alvilda shall stay by you for the rest of your life, and when you die she shall carry you in her arms to the country of Walhalla, where you shall forge golden armour and fashion drinking horns for the gods."

When Freya had spoken, she beckoned to the green maiden, who held in her hand a root and a knife. She cut pieces off the root and laid them on Wayland's feet, and on his eye, then, placing some leaves from her garland over the whole, she breathed gently on it. "Eyr the physician has healed me," cried Wayland, and the fairies took him in their arms and bore him across the waves to a bower in the forest, where he dreamed that Alvilda and Slagfid and Eigil were all bending over him.

When he woke Alvilda was indeed there, and he seemed to catch glimpses of his brothers amid the leaves of the trees. "Arise, my husband," said Alvilda, "and go straight to the Court of Nidud. He still sleeps, and knows nothing. Throw this mantle on your shoulders, and they will take you for his servant."

So Wayland went, and reached the royal chamber, and in his sleep the King trembled, though he knew not that Wayland was near. "Awake," cried Wayland, and the King awoke, and asked who had dared to disturb him thus.

"Be not angry," answered Wayland; "had you slain Wayland long ago, this misfortune that I have to tell you of would never have happened."

"Do not name his name," said the King, "since he sent me those drinking cups a burning fever has laid hold upon me."

"They were not shells, as he told you," answered Wayland, "but the skulls of your two sons, Sir King. Their bodies you will find in Wayland's tower. As for your daughter, she is tossing, bound, on the wild waves of the sea. But now I, Wayland, have come to give you your deathblow——" But before he could draw his sword fear had slain the King yet more quickly.

So Wayland went back to Alvilda, and they went into another country, where he became a famous smith, and he lived to a good old age; and when he died he was carried to Walhalla, as Freya had promised.

# SOME ADVENTURES OF WILLIAM SHORT NOSE.

# PART I.

William Short Nose was also styled William of Orange, quite a different man from the one who came to be King of England, although they both took their title from the same small town in the South of France. This William of Orange spent his life battling with the Saracens in the south of France, and a very hard task he had, for their numbers seemed endless, and as fast as one army was beaten another was gathered together.

Now by a great effort the Saracens had been driven back to the south in the year 732, but before a hundred years had passed they had again crossed the Pyrenees and were streaming over France, south of the Loire, and, what was worse, the men of Gascony were rising too.

Some one had to meet the enemy and crush the rebels, and of all the subjects of King Louis no one was so fit to lead the army of the Franks as William Short Nose, husband of the Lady Gibourc.

It was at the Aliscans that he met them, and a great host they were, spreading over the country till whichever way you looked you saw men flocking round the Golden Dragon, which was the banner of the Saracens.

But it was not Count William's way to think about numbers, and he ordered his trumpeters to sound the charge. Spurring his horse, he dashed from one part of the fight to the other, striking and killing as he went, and heeding as little the wounds that he got as those that he gave, and *they* were many.

The Franks whom he led followed after him, and slew the Saracens as they came on; but the Christians were in comparison but a handful, and their enemies as the sands of the sea.

The young warriors whom William had brought with him were prisoners or dying men, and from far he saw Vivian, whom he loved the best, charging a multitude with his naked sword. "Montjoie! Montjoie!" cried he, "O Bertrand, my cousin, come to my aid!"

Bertrand heard and pressed to his side. "Ride to the river," he said, "and I will protect you with my life"; but Vivian was too weak even to sit on his horse, and fell half fainting at Bertrand's feet.

At this moment there rode at them a large troop of Saracens, headed by their King, Haucebier, and the Christian Knights knew that all was lost. "It is too late now for me to think of life," said Vivian, "but I will die fighting," and again they faced their enemies till Bertrand's horse was killed under him. Then Vivian seized the horse of a dead Saracen, and thrust the bridle into Bertrand's hand, "Fly, for God's sake, it is your only chance. Where is my uncle? If he is dead we have lost the battle."

But Bertrand did not fly, though every instant made the danger more deadly. "If I forsake you, if I take flight," he said, "I shall bring eternal shame upon myself."

"No, no," cried Vivian, "seek my uncle down there in the Aliscans, and bring him to my aid."

"Never till my sword breaks," answered Bertrand, and laid about him harder than ever. And to their joy they heard a war cry sounding in their ears, and five Frankish Counts, cousins of Vivian and of Bertrand, galloped up. Fight they did with all their might, but none fought like Vivian. "Heavens! what a warrior!" cried the Counts as they saw his blows, while the Saracens asked themselves if the man whom they had killed at mid-day had been brought back to life by the help of fiends. "If we let them escape now we shall be covered with shame," said they, "but ere night falls William shall acknowledge that he is conquered."

"Indeed!" said Bertrand, and with his cousins he fell upon them till they fled.

The Counts were victors on this field, but, wounded and weary as they were, another combat lay before them, for a force of twenty thousand Saracens was advancing from the valley.

Their hearts never failed them, but they had no strength left; the young Counts were all taken prisoners, except Vivian, who was left for dead by the side of a fountain where he had been struck down. "O Father in Heaven," he said, feeling his life going from him, "forgive me my sins, and help my uncle, if it is Thy holy will."

William Short Nose was still fighting, though he knew that the victory lay with the Saracens and their hosts. "We are beaten," he said to the fourteen faithful comrades who stood by him. "Listen as you will, no sound of our war cry can be heard. But by the Holy Rood, the Saracens shall know no rest while I am alive. I will give my forefathers no cause for shame, and the minstrels shall not tell in their songs how I fell back before the enemy."

They then gave battle once more, and fought valiantly, till all lay dead upon the ground, save only William himself.

# PART II.

Now the Count knew that if the Saracens were ever to be vanquished and beaten out of fair France he must take heed of his own life, for the task was his and no other man's; so he turned his horse's head towards Orange, and then stopped, for he saw a troop of freshly landed Saracens approaching him along the same road.

"The whole world is full of these Saracens!" he cried in anger, "God alone can save me. My good horse," added he, "you are very tired. If you had had only five days' rest, I would have led you to the charge; but I see plainly that I can get no help from you, and I cannot blame you for it, as you have served me well all day, and for this I thank you greatly. If ever we reach Orange you shall wear no saddle for twenty days, your food shall be the finest corn, and you shall drink out of a golden trough."

And the horse understood; he threw up his head, and pawed the ground, and his strength came back to him as of old. At this sight William Short Nose felt more glad than if he had been given fourteen cities.

No sooner had he entered a valley that led along the road to Orange, than he saw a fresh body of Saracens blocking one end. He turned to escape into another path, but in front of him rode a handful of his enemies. "By the faith that I swore to my dear Lady Gibourc," he said, "I had better die than never strike a blow," and so rode straight at their leader. "William!" cried the Saracen, "this time you will not escape me." But the sun was in his eyes, and his sword missed his aim. Before he could strike another blow William had borne him from his horse and galloped away.

The mountain that he was climbing now was beset with enemies, like all the rest, and William looked in vain for a way of escape. He jumped from his horse and rubbed his flanks saying to him, "What will you do? Your sides are bleeding, and you can scarcely stand; but remember, if once you fall it means my death."

At these words the good horse neighed, pricked up his ears and shook himself, and as he did so the blood seemed to flow strongly in his veins, as of old. Then the count rode down into the field of the Aliscans, and found his nephew, Vivian, lying under a tree.

"Ah!" cried William, "what sorrow for me! To the end of my life I shall mourn this day. Lady Gibourc, await me no longer, for never more shall I return to Orange!"

So he lamented, grieving sore, till Vivian spoke to him. The Count was full of joy to hear his words, and, kneeling beside the youth, took him in his arms, and bade him confess his sins to him, as to his own father. One by one Vivian remembered them all, then a mist floated before his eyes, and, murmuring a farewell to the Lady Gibourc, his soul left the world.

VIVIAN'S LAST CONFESSION

# Vivian's last confession

William laid him gently down on his shield, took another shield for covering, and turned to mount his horse, but at this his heart failed him.

"Is it you, William, that men look to as their leader, who will do this cowardly deed?" he said to himself, and he went back to his nephew's side, and lifted the body on to his horse, to bury it in his city of Orange.

He had done what he could to give honour to Vivian, but he might as well, after all, have left him where he fell, for in a fierce combat with some Saracens on the road the Count was forced to abandon his nephew's body and fight for his own life. He knew the two Saracens well as brave men, but he soon slew one, and the other he unhorsed after a struggle.

"Come back, come back," cried the Saracen; "sell me your horse, for never did I behold his like! I will give you for him twice his weight in gold, and set free besides all your nephews that have been taken prisoners." But William loved his horse, and would not have parted with him to Charles himself.

At length, after fighting nearly every step of the way, he saw the towers of Orange before him, and his palace, Gloriette, where dwelt his wife, the Lady Gibourc. "Ah, with what joy did I leave these walls," he said to himself, "and how many noble Knights have I lost since then! Oh, Gibourc, my wife, will you not go mad when you hear the tidings I have brought!" And, overcome with grief, the Count bowed his head on the neck of his horse.

# PART III.

When he recovered himself he rode straight to the City Gate, and commanded the porter to let him in. "Let down the drawbridge," called he, "and be quick, for time presses." But he forgot that he had changed his own arms, and had taken instead those of a Saracen; therefore the porter, seeing a man with a shield and pennon and helmet that were strange to him, thought he was an enemy, and stood still where he was. "Begone!" he said to William, "if you approach one step nearer I will deal you a blow that will unhorse you! Begone, I tell you, and as quick as you can, or when William Short Nose returns from the Aliscans it will be the worse for you."

"Fear nothing, friend," replied the Count, "for I am William himself. I went to the Aliscans to fight the Saracens, and to help Vivian; but all my men are dead, and I only am left to bring these evil tidings. So open the gates, for the Saracens are close behind."

"You must wait a moment," answered the porter, and he quitted the turret and hastened to the Lady Gibourc. "Noble Countess," cried he, "there knocks at the drawbridge a Knight in Pagan armour, who seems fresh from battle, for his arms are bloody. He is tall of stature and bears himself proudly, and he says he is William Short Nose. I pray you, my lady, come with me and see him for yourself."

The face of Gibourc grew red when she heard the porter's words, and she left the Palace and mounted the battlements, where she called, "Warrior, what is your will?"

"Oh, lady," answered he, "open the gate, and that quickly. Twenty thousand Saracens are close upon my track; if they reach me, I am a dead man."

"You cannot enter," replied Gibourc. "I am alone here except for this porter, a priest, a few children, and some ladies whose husbands are all at the war. Neither gate nor wicket will be opened until the return of my beloved lord, William the Count." Then William bowed his head for a moment, and tears ran down his cheeks.

"My lady, I am William himself," said he. "Do you not know me?"

"Saracen, you lie," replied Gibourc. "Take off your helmet and let me see who you are!"

"Noble Countess," cried he, "this is no time to parley. Look round you! Is not every hill covered with enemies?"

"Ah, now I know you are not William," answered she, "for all the Saracens in the world would never have stirred him with fear. By St. Peter! neither gate nor wicket shall be opened till I have seen your face. I am alone and must defend myself. The voices of many men are alike."

Then the Count lifted his helmet: "Lady look and be content. I am William himself. Now let me in."

Gibourc knew that it was indeed the Count who had returned, and was about to order the gates to be opened when there appeared in sight a troop of Saracens escorting two hundred prisoners, all of them young Knights, and thirty ladies with fair, white faces. Each one was loaded with chains, and cowered under the blows of their captors. Their cries and prayers for mercy reached the ears of Gibourc, and, changing her mind, she said quickly: "There is the proof that you are not William, my husband, whose fame has spread far! For he would never have suffered his brethren to be so shamefully entreated while he was by!"

"Heavens!" cried the Count, "to what hard tests does she put me! But if I lose my head I will do her bidding, for what is there that I would *not* do for the love of God and of her!"

# PART IV.

Without a word more he turned, and spurred his horse at the Saracens. So sudden and fierce was his attack that the foremost riders fell back on those behind, who were thrown into confusion, while William's sword swept him a path to the centre, where the prisoners stood bound. The Saracens expected the city gates to open and a body of Franks to come forth to destroy them, and without waiting another moment they turned and fled.

# The Captives—William Short-nose rides to the rescue

"Oh, fair lord," called Gibourc, who from the battlements had watched the fight, "come back, come back, for now indeed you may enter." And William heard her voice, and left the Saracens to go where they would while he struck the chains off the prisoners, and led them to the gates of Orange, when he himself rode back to the Saracens.

Not again would the Lady Gibourc have reason to call him coward.

And Gibourc saw, and her heart swelled within her, and she repented her of her words. "It is my fault if he is slain,", she wept. "Oh, come back, come back!"

And William came.

Now the drawbridge was let down, and he entered the city followed by the Christians whom he had delivered, and the Countess unlaced his helmet, and bathed his wounds, and then stopped, doubting.

"You cannot be William after all," said she, "for William would have brought back the young kinsmen who went with him; and would have been encircled by minstrels singing the great deeds he had done."

"Ah, noble Countess, you speak truth," answered he. "Henceforth my life will be spent in mourning, for my friends and comrades who went to war with me are lying dead at the Aliscan."

Great was the sorrow in the city of Orange and in the palace of her lord, where the ladies of the Countess mourned for their husbands. But it was Gibourc who first roused herself from her grief for Vivian and others whom she had loved well. "Noble Count," she said, "do not lose your courage. Remember it is not near Orleans, in safety, that your lands lie, but in the very midst of the Saracens. Orange never will have peace till they are subdued. So send messengers to King Louis, and to your father, Aimeri, asking for aid."

"Heavens!" cried William, "has the world ever seen so wise a lady?"

"Let no one turn you from your road," she went on. "At the news of your distress all the Barons that are your kin will fly to your help. Their numbers are as the sands of the sea."

"But how shall I make them believe in what has befallen us?" answered William. "If I do not go myself I will send nobody, and go myself I will not, for I will not leave you alone again for all the gold in Pavia."

"Sir, you must go," said Gibourc, weeping. "I will stay here with my ladies, and each will place a helmet on her head, and hang a shield round her neck, and buckle a sword to her side, and with the help of the Knights whom you have delivered, we shall know how to defend ourselves."

William's heart bounded at her words; he took her in his arms, and promised that he himself would go, and that he would never lie soft till he returned again to Orange.

# PART V.

Thus William Short Nose set forth and the next day passed through Orleans. There he met with his brother Ernaut, who had ridden home from escorting King Louis back to Paris. Ernaut promised his help and that of his father and brothers, but counselled William to go to Laon, where a great feast would be held and many persons would be assembled. The Count followed Ernaut's counsel, but refused the troop of Knights which Ernaut offered him, liking rather to ride alone.

He made his entrance into Laon, and the people laughed at him and made jests on his tall, thin horse; but William let them laugh, and rode on until he reached the Palace. There he alighted under an olive tree, and, fastening his horse to one of the branches, took off his helmet and unbuckled his breastplate. The people stared as they passed by, but nobody spoke to him.

Someone told the King that a strange man without even a squire was sitting before the Palace under an olive tree. The King's face grew dark as he heard their tale, for he loved to keep his gardens for his own pleasure. "Sanson," he called to one of his guards, "go and find out who this stranger is and whence he comes, but beware of bringing him hither."

Sanson hastened to do his errand, and William answered, "My name is one that is known to France. I am William Short Nose, and I come from Orange. My body is worn out with much riding; I pray you hold my horse until I have spoken to King Louis."

"Noble Count," replied Sanson, "let me first return to the King and tell him who you are. And be not angry, I beseech you, for such are my orders."

"Be quick, then, my friend," said William, "and do not neglect to tell the King that I am in great distress. This is the time to show his love for me; and if he truly does love me, let him come to meet me with the great lords of his Court. If he does not come, I have no other hope."

"I will tell him what you say," said Sanson, "and if it rests with me you shall be content."

Then Sanson went back to the King. "It is William, the famous William!" he said, "and he wishes you to go out to meet him."

"Never!" answered Louis; "will he always be a thorn in my side! Woe be to him who rejoices at his coming."

So the King sat still, and on the steps of the Palace there gathered Knights and Nobles in goodly numbers, and hardly one but wore a helmet set with precious stones, a sword or a shield which had been given him by William himself. But now they were rich and he was poor, so they mocked at him.

"My lords," said William, "you do ill to treat me so. I have loved you all, and you bear the tokens of my love about you at this moment. If I can give you no more gifts, it is because I have lost all I have in the world at the Aliscans. My men are dead, and my nephews are prisoners in the hands of the Saracens. It is the Lady Gibourc who bade me come here, and it is she who asks for help through me. Have pity on us, and help us." But without a word, they rose up and went into the Palace, and William knew what their love was worth.

The young men told Louis of the words that the Count had spoken, and the King rose and leaned out of the window. "Sir William," said he, "go to the inn, and let them bathe your horse. You seem in a sorry plight, without a groom to help you."

William heard and vowed vengeance. But if the King and the courtiers had no hearts, in his need a friend came to him, Guimard, a citizen of Laon, who took the Count home and offered him rich food. But because of his vow to the Lady Gibourc, he would only eat coarse bread, and drink water from the spring; and as soon as it was light he rose up from his bed of fresh hay, and dressed himself. "Where are you going," asked his host.

"To the Palace, to entreat the aid of the King, and woe be to him who tries to stop me."

"May God protect you, Sir," answered Guimard. "To-day the King crowns Blanchefleur, your sister, who no doubt loves you well. And he gives her for her dower the richest land in all fair France, but a land that is never at peace."

"Well," said William, "I will be present at the ceremony. Indeed they cannot do without me, for all France is under my care, and it is my right to bear her standard in battle. And let them beware how they move me to wrath, lest I depose the King of France and tear the crown from his head."

The Count placed a breastplate under his jerkin, and hid his sword under his cloak. The gates of the Palace opened before him and he entered the vaulted hall. It was filled with the greatest nobles in the land, and ladies with rich garments of silk and gold. Lords and ladies both knew him, but not one gave him welcome—not even his sister, the Queen. His fingers played with his sword, and he had much ado not to use it. But while his wrath was yet kindling the heralds announced that his father, Aimeri, had come.

# PART VI.

The Lord of Narbonne stepped on to the grass with his noble Countess, his four sons, and many servants. King Louis and the Queen hastened to meet them, and amid cries of joy they mounted the steps into the hall. Aimeri sat beside the King, and the Countess was seated next the Queen, while the Knights placed themselves on the floor of the hall. And William sat also, but alone and apart, nursing his anger.

At last he rose, and, advancing to the middle of the floor, he said with a loud voice: "Heaven protect my mother, my father, my brothers and my friends; but may His curse alight on my sister and on the King, who have left me to be the butt of all the mockers of the Court. By all the Saints! were not my father sitting next to him, this sword should ere now have cloven his skull." The King listened pale with fright, and the rest whispered to each other, "William is angry, something will happen!"

When Ermengarde and Aimeri saw their son standing before them great joy filled their souls. They left their seats and flung themselves on his neck, and William's brother also ran to greet him. The Count told them how he had been vanquished at the Aliscans, and he himself had fled to Orange, and of the distress in which he had left Gibourc. "It was at her bidding I came here to ask aid from Louis, but from the way he has treated me I see plainly that he has no heart. By St. Peter! he shall repent before I go, and my sister also."

The King heard and again waxed cold with fear; the nobles heard and whispered: "Who is strong enough to compass this matter? No man, be he the bravest in France, ever went to his help and came back to tell the tale."

It was the Lady Ermengarde who broke the silence. "O God," she cried, "to think that the Franks should be such cowards! Have no fear, fair son William, I have still left gold that would fill thirty chariots, and I will give it to those who enrol themselves under your banner."

Aimeri smiled and sighed as he listened to her words, and his sons shed tears.

William answered nothing, but remained standing in the middle of the hall, his eyes fixed on his sister sitting on her throne, with a small golden crown upon her head, and on her husband, King Louis.

"This, then, O King, is the reward of all I have done! When Charlemagne, your father, died, you would have lost your crown if I had not forced the Barons to place it upon your head."

"That is true," answered the King, "and in remembrance of your services I will to-day bestow on you a fief."

"Yes," cried Blanchefleur, "and no doubt will deprive me of one. A nice agreement, truly! Woe to him who dares carry it out."

"Be silent, woman without shame!" said William. "Every word you speak proclaims your baseness! You pass your days eating and drinking, and little you care that we endure heat and cold, hunger and thirst, and suffer wounds and death so that your life may be easy."

Then he bounded forwards, and, drawing his sword, would have cut off her head had not Ermengarde wrenched the weapon from his hands. Before he could seize it again the Queen darted away and took refuge in her chamber, where she fell fainting on the floor.

# PART VII.

It was her daughter Alix, the fair and the wise, who raised her up and then heard with shame the tale she had to tell. "How could you speak so to my uncle, the best man that ever wore a sword?" asked Alix. "It was he who made you Queen of France."

"Yes, my daughter, you say truth," answered the Queen, "I have done ill, I will make peace with my brother;" and she wept over her wicked speech, while Alix, red and white as the roses in May, went down into the hall, where the Franks were still whispering together, and calling curses on the head of William.

They all rose as the maiden entered; Aimeri, her grandfather, took her in his arms, and her four uncles kissed her cheek. Her presence seemed to calm the anger and trouble which before had reigned throughout the hall, and Ermengarde flung herself at William's feet and besought his pardon for the Queen.

William raised his mother from her knees, but his anger was not soothed. "I have no love for the King," he said, "and before night I will break his pride," and he stood, his face red with wrath, leaning on his naked sword.

Not a sound was heard, and the eyes of all were fixed breathlessly upon William. Then in her turn Alix stepped forward and knelt at his feet. "Punish me in my mother's place," said she, "and cut off my head if you will, but let there be peace, I pray you, between you and my father and mother."

At the voice of Alix William's wrath melted, but at first he would promise nothing. "Fair son William," said Ermengarde again, "be content. The King will do what you desire, and will aid you to the uttermost."

The Lady Alix Stays the wrath of William Shortnose

# The Lady Alix stays the wrath of William Shortnose

"Yes, I will aid you," answered the King.

So peace was made, the Queen was fetched, and they all sat down to a great feast. In this manner the pride of the King was broken.

But when one man is shifty and another is hasty, wrath is not apt to slumber long, and treaties of peace are easier made than kept. When the feast was over William pressed King Louis to prepare an army at once; but the King would bind himself to nothing. "We will speak of it again," said he; "I will tell you to-morrow whether I will go or not."

At this William grew red with rage, and holding out a wand he said to the King, "I give you back your fief. I will take nothing from you, and henceforth will neither be your friend nor your vassal."

"Keep your fief," said Ernaut to his brother, "and leave the King to do as he will. I will help you and my brothers also, and between us we shall have twenty thousand men to fight with any Saracens we shall find."

"You speak weak words," cried Aimeri; "he is Seneschal of France, and also her Standard Bearer; he has a right to our help." And Alix approved of his saying, and the Queen likewise. The King saw that none were on his side and dared refuse no longer. "Count William, for love of you I will call together my army, and a hundred thousand men shall obey your commands. But I myself will not go with you, for my kingdom needs me badly."

"Remain, Sire," answered William, "I myself will lead the host." And the King sent out his messengers, and soon a vast army was gathered under the walls of Laon.

# PART VIII.

It was on one of these days, when the Count stood in the great hall, that there entered from the kitchen a young man whom he had never seen before. The youth, whose name was Rainouart, was tall, strong as a wild boar, and swift as a deer. The scullions and grooms had played off jests upon him during the night, but had since repented them sorely, for he had caught the leaders up in his arms and broken their heads against the walls.

The rest, eager to avenge their comrades' death, prepared to overcome him with numbers, and in spite of his strength it might have gone ill with Rainouart had not Aimeri de Narbonne, hearing the noise, forbade more brawling.

Count William was told of the unseemly scuffle, and asked the King who and what the young man was who could keep at bay so many of his fellows. "I bought him once at sea," said Louis, "and paid a hundred marks for him. They pretend that he is the son of a Saracen, but he will never reveal the name of his father. Not knowing what to do with him, I sent him to the kitchen."

"Give him to me, King Louis," said William, smiling, "I promise you he shall have plenty to eat."

"Willingly," answered the King.

Far off in the kitchen Rainouart was chafing at the sound of the horses' hoofs, and at the scraps of talk let fall by the Knights, who were seeing to the burnishing of their armour before they started to fight the Saracens. "To think," he said to himself, "that I, who am of right King of Spain, should be loitering here, heaping logs on the fire and skimming the pot. But let King Louis look to himself! Before a year is past I will snatch the crown from his head."

When the army was ready to march he made up his mind what to do, and it was thus that he sought out William in the great hall. "Noble Count, let me come with you, I implore you. I can help to look after the horses and cook the food, and if at any time blows are needed I can strike as well as any man."

"Good fellow," answered William, who wished to try what stuff he was made of, "how could you, who have passed your days in the kitchen, sleeping on the hearth when you were not busy turning the spit—how could you bear all the fatigue of war, the long fasts, and the longer watches? Before a month had passed you would be dead by the roadside!"

"Try me," said he, "and if you will not have me I will go alone, and fight barefoot. My only weapon will be an iron-bound staff, and it shall kill as many Saracens as the best sword among you all."

"Come then," answered the Count.

# PART IX.

The next morning the army set forth, and Alix and the Queen watched them go from the steps of the Palace. When Alix saw Rainouart stepping proudly along with his heavy staff on his shoulder her heart stirred, and she said to her mother, "See, what a goodly young man! In the whole army there is not one like him! Let me bid him farewell, for nevermore shall I see his match."

"Peace! my daughter," answered the Queen, "I hope indeed that he may never more return to Laon." Alix took no heed of her mother's words, but signed to Rainouart to draw near. Then she put her arms round his neck, and said, "Brother, you have been a long time at Court, and now you are going to fight under my uncle's banner. If ever I have given you pain, I ask your pardon." After that she kissed him, and bade him go.

*PART IX.*

111. ALIX KISSES RAINOUART.

# Alix kisses Rainouart

At Orleans William took leave of his father and his mother, who returned to their home at Narbonne; and also of his brothers, who promised to return to meet William under the walls of Orange, which they did faithfully.

He pressed on with his army quickly till he came in sight of his native city. But little of it could he see, for a great smoke covered all the land, rising up from the burning towers which the Saracens had that morning set on fire. Enter the city they could not, for Gibourc and her ladies held it firm, and, armed with helmets and breastplates, flung stones upon the enemy.

When William beheld the smoke, and whence it came, he cried: "Orange is burning! Gibourc is carried captive! To arms! To arms!" And he spurred his horse, Rainouart running by his side.

From her tower Gibourc saw through the smoke a thousand banners waving and the sparkle of armour, and heard the sound of the horses' hoofs, and it seemed to her that the Saracens were drawing near anew. "O William!" cried she, "have you really forgotten me? Noble Count, you linger overlong! Never more shall I look upon your face." And so saying she fell fainting on the floor.

But something stirred the pulses of Gibourc, and she soon sat up again, and there at the gate was William, with Rainouart behind him. "Fear nothing, noble lady," said he, "it is the army of France that I have brought with me. Open, and welcome to us!"

The news seemed so good to Gibourc that she could not believe it, and she bade the Count unlace his helmet, so that she might indeed be sure that it was he. William did her bidding, then she ran swiftly to the gate and let down the drawbridge, and William stepped across it and embraced her tenderly. Then he ordered his army to take up its quarters in the city.

# PART X.

Gibourc's eyes had fallen upon Rainouart, who had passed her on his way to the kitchen, where he meant to leave his stout wooden staff. "Tell me," said she to the Count, "who is the young man who bears lightly on his shoulder that huge piece of wood which would weigh down a horse? He is handsome and well made. Where did you find him?"

"Lady," answered William, "he was given me by the King."

"My Lord," said Gibourc, "be sure you see that he is honourably treated. He looks to me to be of high birth. Has he been baptised?"

"No, Madam, he is not a Christian. He was brought from Spain as a child, and kept for seven years in the kitchen. But take him, I pray you, under your protection, and do with him as you will."

The Count was hungry, and while waiting for dinner to be served he stood with Gibourc at the windows which looked out beyond the city. An army was drawing near; thousands of men, well mounted and freshly equipped. "Gibourc!" cried the Count joyfully, "here is my brother Ernaut with his vassals. Now all the Saracens in the world shall not prevent Bertrand from being delivered to-morrow."

On all sides warriors began to arrive, led by the fathers of those who had been taken prisoners with Bertrand, and with them came Aimeri and the brothers of William. Glad was the heart of the Count as he bade them welcome to his Palace, and ordered a feast to be made ready, and showed each Knight where he should sit.

It was late before the supper was served, but when every man had his trencher filled Rainouart entered the hall, armed with his staff, and stood leaning against a pillar, watching the noble company. "Sir," said Aimeri, the man whom the Saracens most dreaded, "who is it that I see standing there holding a piece of wood that five peasants could hardly lift? Does he mean to murder us?"

"That youth," replied William, "is a gift to me from King Louis. None living is as strong as he." Then Aimeri called Rainouart, and bade him sit at his side, and eat and drink as he would. "Noble Count," said Aimeri, "such men grow not on every bush. Keep him and cherish him, and bring him with you to the Aliscans. For with his staff he will slay many Pagans."

"Yes," answered Rainouart, "wherever I appear the Pagans will fall dead at the sight of me." Aimeri and William laughed to hear him, but ere four days were past they had learned what he was worth.

# PART XI.

Rainouart went back to the kitchen and slept soundly, but as he had drunk much wine the cooks and scullions thought to play jokes upon him, and lighted some wooden shavings with which to burn his moustache. At the first touch of the flame Rainouart leapt to his feet, seized the head cook by his legs, flung him on to the blazing fire, and turned for another victim, but they had all fled.

At daybreak they went to William to pray for vengeance on the murderer of the cook. If the Count would not forbid him the kitchen, not a morsel of food would they cook. But William only laughed at their threats, and said, "Beware henceforth how you meddle with Rainouart. Did I not forbid anyone to mock at him, and do you dare to disobey my orders? Lady Gibourc, take Rainouart to your chamber, and keep him beside you."

So the Countess went to the kitchen and found Rainouart sitting on a bench, his head leaning against his staff. She sat down by him and said graciously, "Brother, come with me and we will have some talk together."

"THE LADY GIBOURC, WITH RAINOUART IN THE KITCHEN"

# The Lady Gibourc with Rainouart in the kitchen

"Willingly," answered Rainouart, "the more so that I can hardly keep my hands off these scoundrels."

He followed Gibourc to her room, and then she questioned him about his childhood.

"Have you brothers or sisters?" asked she.

"Yes," he answered, "beyond the sea I have a brother who is a King, and a sister who is more beautiful than a fairy," and as he spoke he bent his head. Something in her heart told Gibourc that this might be her brother, but she only asked again, "Where do you come from?"

"Lady," he replied, "I will answer that question the day I come back from the battle which William shall have won, thanks to my aid."

Gibourc kept silence, but she opened a chest and drew from it a white breastplate that had belonged to her uncle, which was so finely wrought that no sword could pierce it; likewise a helmet of steel and a sword that could cut through iron more easily than a scythe cuts grass. "My friend," she said, "buckle this sword to your side. It may be useful to you."

Rainouart took the sword and drew it from its scabbard, but it seemed so light that he threw it down again. "Lady," he cried, "what good can such a plaything do me? But with my staff between my hands there is not a Pagan that can stand up against me, and if one escapes then let Count William drive me from his door."

At this Gibourc felt sure this was indeed her brother, but she did not yet like to ask him more questions, and in her joy she began to weep. "Lady," said Rainouart, "do not weep. As long as my staff is whole William shall be safe."

"My friend, may Heaven protect you," she answered, "but a man without armour is soon cut down; so take these things and wear them in battle," and she laced on the helmet, and buckled the breastplate, and fastened the sword on his thigh. "If your staff breaks, it may serve you," said she.

Rainouart was proud indeed when the armour was girded on him, and he sat himself down well pleased at William's table. The Knights vied with each other in pouring him out bumpers of wine, and after dinner every man tried to lift his iron-bound staff, but none could raise it from the ground, except William himself, who by putting forth all his strength lifted it the height of a foot.

"Let me aid you," said Rainouart, and he whirled it round his head, throwing it lightly from hand to hand. "We are wasting time," he said. "I fear lest the Saracens should fly before we come up with them. If I only have the chance to make them feel the weight of my staff, I will soon sweep the battlefield." And William embraced him for these words, and ordered the trumpets to be sounded and the army to march.

From her window Gibourc watched them go. She saw the Knights stream out into the plain, their banners floating on the wind, their helmets shining in the sun, their shields glittering with gold. She heard their horses neigh, and she prayed God to bless all this noble host.

# PART XII.

After two days' march they came within sight of the Aliscans, but for five miles round the country was covered by the Saracen army. William saw that some of his men quailed at the number of the foe, so he turned and spoke to his soldiers. "My good lords," he said, "a fearful battle awaits us, and we must not give way an inch. If any man feels afraid let him go back to his own land. This is no place for cowards."

The cowards heard joyfully, and without shame took the road by which they had come. They spurred their horses and thought themselves safe, but they rejoiced too soon.

At the mouth of a bridge Rainouart met them, and when he saw that they were part of the Christian host he raised his staff and barred their passage. "Where are you going?" asked he. "To France, for rest," answered the cowards; "the Count has dismissed us, and when we reach our homes we shall see to the rebuilding of our castles, which have fallen into ill-repair during the wars. Come with us, if you are a wise man."

"Ask some one else," said Rainouart; "Count William has given me the command of the army, and it is to him that I have to render account. Do you think I shall let you run away like hares?" And, swinging his staff round his head, he laid about him.

Struck dumb with terror at the sight of their comrades falling rapidly round them, they cried with one voice, "Sir Rainouart, we will return and fight with you."

PART XII.

# Rainouart stops the cowards

So they turned their horses' heads and rode the way they had come, and Rainouart followed, keeping guard over them with his staff. When they reached the army he went straight to William, and begged that he might have the command of them. "I will change them into a troop of lions," said he.

Harsh words and gibes greeted the cowards, but Rainouart soon forced the mockers to silence. "Leave my men alone!" he cried, "or by the faith I owe to Gibourc I will make you. I am a King's son, and the time has come to show you what manner of man I am. I have idled long, but I will idle no longer. I am of the blood royal, and the saying is true that good blood cannot lie."

"How well he speaks!" whispered the Franks to each other, for they dared not let their voices be heard.

# PART XIII.

Now the battle was to begin, for the two armies were drawn up in fighting array, and Rainouart took his place at the head of his cowards opposite the Saracens, from which race he sprang.

The charge was sounded, and the two armies met with a shock, and many a man fell from his horse and was trampled under foot. "Narbonne! Narbonne!" shouted Aimeri, advancing within reach of a crossbow shot, and he would have been slain had not his sons dashed to his rescue. Count William did miracles, and the Saracens were driven so far back that Rainouart feared the battle would be ended before he had struck a blow.

Followed by his troop of cowards Rainouart made straight for the enemy, and before him they fell as corn before a sickle. "Strike, soldiers," shouted he; "strike and avenge the noble Vivian."

Rainouart and his cowards pressed on and on, and the Saracens fell back, step by step, till they reached the sea, where their ships were anchored.

Then Rainouart drove his staff in the sand, and by its help swung himself on board a small vessel, which happened to be the very one in which the nephews of William were imprisoned. He laid about him right and left with his staff, till he had slain all the gaolers, and at last he came to a young man whose eyes were bandaged and his feet tied together. "Who are you?" asked Rainouart.

"I am Bertrand, nephew of William Short Nose. Four months ago I was taken captive by the Saracens, and if, as I think, they carry me into Arabia, then may God have pity on my soul, for it is all over with my body."

"Sir Count," answered Rainouart, "for love of William I will deliver you."

Seizing the weapons of the dead Saracens, they scrambled on shore, and, while fighting for their lives, looked about for their uncle, whom they knew at last by the sweep of his sword, which kept a clear space around him. More than once Rainouart swept back fresh foes that were pressing forwards, till the tide of battle carried him away and brought him opposite Desramé the King. "Who are you?" asked Desramé, struck by his face, for there was nothing royal in his dress or his arms.

"I am Rainouart, vassal of William whom I love, and if you do hurt to him I will do hurt to you also."

"Rainouart, I am your father," cried Desramé, and he besought him to forswear Christianity and to become a follower of Mahomet; but Rainouart turned a deaf ear, and challenged him to continue the combat. Desramé was no match for his son, and was soon struck from his horse. "Oh, wretch that I am," said Rainouart to himself, "I have slain my brothers and wounded my father—it is my staff which has done all this evil," and he flung it far from him. He would have been wiser to have kept it, for in a moment three giants surrounded him, and he had only his fists with which to beat them back. Suddenly his hand touched the sword buckled on him by Gibourc, which he had forgotten, and he drew it from its scabbard, and with three blows clove the heads of the giants in twain. Meanwhile King Desramé took refuge in the only ship that had not been sunk by the Christians, and spread its sails. "Come back whenever you like, fair father," called Rainouart after him.

# PART XIV.

The fight was over; the Saracens acknowledged that they were beaten, and the booty they had left behind them was immense. The army, wearied with the day's toil, lay down to sleep, but before midnight Rainouart was awake and trumpets called to arms. "Vivian must be buried," said he, "and then the march to Orange will begin."

Rainouart rode at the head, his sword drawn, prouder than a lion; and as he went along a poor peasant threw himself before him, asking for vengeance on some wretches who had torn up a field of beans, which was all he had with which to feed his family. Rainouart ordered the robbers to be brought before him and had them executed. Then he gave to the peasant their horses and their armour in payment of the ruined beans. "Ah, it has turned out a good bargain for me," said the peasant. "Blessed be the hour when I sowed such a crop."

William entered into his Palace, where a great feast was spread for the visitors, but one man only remained outside the walls and that was Rainouart, of whom no one thought in the hour of triumph. His heart swelled with bitterness as he thought of the blows he had given, and the captives he had set free, and, weeping with anger, he turned his face towards the Aliscans.

On the road some Knights met him, and asked him whither he was going and why he looked so sad. Then his wrath and grief burst out, and he told how he mourned that ever he had slain a man in William's cause, and that he was now hastening to serve under the banner of Mahomet, and would shortly return with a hundred thousand men behind him, and would avenge himself on France and her King. Only towards Alix would he show any pity!

In vain the Knights tried to soften his heart, it was too sore to listen. So they rode on fast to Orange and told the Count what Rainouart had said.

"I have done him grievous wrong," answered William, and ordered twenty Knights to ride after him. But the Knights were received with threats and curses, and came back to Orange faster than they had left it, thinking that Rainouart was at their heels.

William smiled when he heard the tale of his messengers, and bade them bring his horse, and commanded that a hundred Knights should follow him, and prayed Gibourc to ride at his side. They found Rainouart entering a vessel whose sails were already spread, and all William's entreaties would have availed nothing had not Gibourc herself implored his forgiveness.

"I am your brother," cried Rainouart, throwing himself on her neck; "I may confess it now, and for your sake I will pardon the Count's ingratitude, and never more will I remind you of it."

There was great joy in Orange when William rode through the gates with Rainouart beside him, and the next day the Count made him his Seneschal, and he was baptised. Then William sent his brothers on an embassy to the King in Paris, to beg that he would bestow the hand of Princess Alix on Rainouart, son of King Desramé and brother of Lady Gibourc. And when the embassy returned Alix returned with it, and the marriage took place with great splendour; but to the end of his life, whenever Rainouart felt cold, he warmed himself in the kitchen.

# THE SWORD EXCALIBUR

## THE SWORD EXCALIBUR 127

King Arthur had fought a hard battle with the tallest Knight in all the land, and though he struck hard and well, he would have been slain had not Merlin enchanted the Knight and cast him into a deep sleep, and brought the King to a hermit who had studied the art of healing, and cured all his wounds in three days. Then Arthur and Merlin waited no longer, but gave the hermit thanks and departed.

As they rode together Arthur said, "I have no sword," but Merlin bade him be patient and he would soon give him one. In a little while they came to a large lake, and in the midst of the lake Arthur beheld an arm rising out of the water, holding up a sword. "Look!" said Merlin, "that is the sword I spoke of." And the King looked again, and a maiden stood upon the water. "That is the Lady of the Lake," said Merlin, "and she is coming to you, and if you ask her courteously she will give you the sword." So when the maiden drew near Arthur saluted her and said, "Maiden, I pray you tell me whose sword is that which an arm is holding out of the water. I wish it were mine, for I have lost my sword."

# Arthur meets the Lady of the Lake and gets the sword Excalibur

"That sword is mine, King Arthur," answered she, "and I will give it to you, if you in return will give me a gift when I ask you."

"By my faith," said the King, "I will give you whatever gift you ask." "Well," said the maiden, "get into the barge yonder, and row yourself to the sword, and take it and the scabbard with you." For this was the sword Excalibur. "As for *my* gift, I will ask it in my own time."

Then King Arthur and Merlin dismounted from their horses and tied them up safely, and went into the barge, and when they came to the place where the arm was holding the sword Arthur took it by the handle, and the arm disappeared. And they brought the sword back to land.

As they rode the King looked lovingly on his sword, which Merlin saw, and, smiling, said, "Which do you like best, the sword or the scabbard?" "I like the sword," answered Arthur. "You are not wise to say that," replied Merlin, "for the scabbard is worth ten of the sword, and as long as it is buckled on you, you will lose no blood, however sorely you may be wounded."

So they rode into the town of Carlion, and Arthur's Knights gave them a glad welcome, and said it was a joy to serve under a King who risked his life as much as any common man.

# HOW GRETTIR THE STRONG BECAME AN OUTLAW.

# I

Now Grettir had a strong wish to go to Norway, for Earl Svein had fled the country after being beaten in a battle, and Olaf the Saint held sole rule as King.

There was also a man named Thorir of Garth who had been in Norway, and was a friend of the King; this man was anxious to send out his sons to become the King's men. The sons accordingly sailed, and came to a haven at Stead, where they remained some days, during stormy weather.

Grettir also had sailed after them, and the crew bore down on Stead, being hard put to it by reason of foul weather, snow and frost; and they were all worn, weary and wet. To save expense they did not put into the harbour, but lay to beside a dyke, where, though perished with cold, they could not light a fire.

As the night wore on they saw that a great fire was burning on the opposite side of the sound up which they had sailed, and fell to talking and wondering whether any man might fetch that fire.

Grettir said little, but made ready for swimming; he had on but a cape and sail-cloth breeches. He girt up the cape and tied a rope strongly round his middle, and had with him a cask; then he leaped overboard and swam across. There he saw a house, and heard much talking and noise, so he turned towards it, and found it to be a house of refuge for coasting sailors; twelve men were inside sitting round a great fire on the floor, drinking, and these were the sons of Thorir.

When Grettir burst in he knew not who was there; he himself seemed huge of bulk, for his cape was frozen all over into ice; therefore the men took him to be some evil troll, and smote at him with anything that lay to hand; but Grettir put all blows aside, snatched up some firebrands, and swam therewith back to the ship. Grettir's comrades were mightily pleased, and bepraised him and his journey and his prowess.

Next morning they crossed the sound, but found no house, only a great heap of ashes, and therein many bones of men. They asked if Grettir had done this misdeed; but he said it had happened even as he had expected.

The men said wherever they came that Grettir had burnt those people; and the news soon spread that the victims were the sons of Thorir of Garth.

Grettir therefore now grew into such bad repute that he was driven from the ship, and scarcely any one would say a good word for him. As matters were so hopeless he determined to explain all to the King, and offer to free himself from the slander by handling hot iron without being burned.

His ill-luck still pursued him, for when all was ready in the Church where the ceremony was about to take place, a wild-looking lad, or, as some said, an unclean spirit, started up from no one knew where, and spoke such impertinent words to Grettir that he felled him with a blow of his fist.

After this the King would not allow the ceremony to go on: "Thou art far too luckless a man to abide with us, and if ever man has been cursed, of all men must thou have been," said he; and advised him to go back to Iceland in the summer.

Meanwhile Asmund the Greyhaired died, and was buried at Biarg, and Atli succeeded to his goods, but was soon afterwards basely murdered by a neighbouring chief, who bore him ill-will for his many friendships, and grudged him his possessions.

Thorir of Garth brought a suit at the Thing to have Grettir outlawed for the burning of his sons; but Skapti the Lawman thought it scarcely fair to condemn a man unheard, and spoke these wise words: "A tale is half told if one man tells it, for most folk are readiest to bring their stories to the worser side when there are two ways of telling them."

Thorir, however, was a man of might, and had powerful friends; these between them pushed on the suit, and with a high hand rather than according to law obtained their decree. Thus was Grettir outlawed for a deed of which he was innocent.

Next, Grettir's enemy Thorir of Garth heard of his whereabouts, and prevailed upon one Thorir Redbeard to attempt to slay him.

So Redbeard laid his plans, with the object, as it is quaintly phrased, of "winning" Grettir. He, however, declined to be "won," for Redbeard fared no better than Grim.

*GRETTIR OVERTHROWS THORIR REDBEARD*

# Grettir overthrows Thorir Redbeard

He tried to slay the outlaw while he was swimming back from his nets, but Grettir sank like a stone and swam along the bottom, till he reached a place where he could land unseen by Redbeard. He then came on him from behind, while Redbeard was still looking for his appearance out of the water; heaved him over his head, and caused him to fall so heavily that his weapon fell out of his hand. Grettir seized it and smote off his head.

# DEATH OF GRETTIR THE STRONG.

# DEATH OF GRETTIR THE STRONG.

About this time, Grettir having been so many years in outlawry, many thought that the sentence should be annulled, and it was deemed certain that he would be pardoned in the next ensuing summer; but they who had owned the island were discontented at the prospect of his acquittal, and urged Angle either to give back the island or slay Grettir.

Now Angle had a foster-mother, Thurid; she was old and cunning in witchcraft, which she had learnt in her youth; for though Christianity had now been established in the island, yet there remained still many traces of heathendom.

Angle and she put out a ten-oared boat to pick a quarrel with Grettir, of which the upshot was that the outlaw threw a huge stone into the boat, where the witch lay covered up with wrappings, and broke her leg. Angle had to endure many taunts at the failure of all his attempts to outplay Grettir.

One day, Thurid was limping along by the sea, when she found a large log, part of the trunk of a tree. She cut a flat space on it, carved magic characters, or runes, on the root, reddened them with her blood, and sang witch-words over them; then she walked backwards round it, and widdershins—which means in a direction against the sun—and thrust the log out to sea under many strong spells, in such wise that it should drive out to Drangey.

In the teeth of the wind it went, till it came to the island, where Illugi and Grettir saw it, but knowing it boded them ill, they thrust it out from shore; yet next morning was it there again, nearer the ladders than before; but again they drove it out to sea.

The days wore on to summer, and a gale sprang up with wet; the brothers being short of firewood, Noise was sent down to the shore to look for drift, grumbling at being ordered out in bad weather, when, lo! the log was there again, and he fetched it up.

Grettir was angry with Noise, and not noticing what the log was, hewed at it with his axe, which glanced from the wood and cut into his leg, right down to the bone.

Illugi bound it up, and at first it seemed as though the wound was healed. But after a time his leg took to paining Grettir, and became blue and swollen, so that he could not sleep, and Illugi watched by him night and day.

At this time Thurid advised Angle to make another attempt on the island; he therefore gathered a force of a dozen men together, and set sail in very foul weather, but no sooner had they reached open sea than the wind lulled, so they came to Drangey at dusk.

Noise had been told to guard the ladders, and had gone out as usual with very ill grace; he thought to himself he would not draw them up, so he lay down there and fell asleep, remaining all day long in slumber till Angle came to the island.

Mounting the ladders, he and his men found Noise snoring at the top; arousing him roughly, they learned from him what had happened, and how Grettir lay sick in the hut with Illugi tending him.

Angle thrashed Noise soundly for betraying his master, and the men made for the hut. Illugi guarded the door with the greatest valour, and when they thrust at him with spears he struck off all the spear heads from the shafts.

But some of the men leapt up on to the roof, tore away the thatch, and broke one of the rafters. Grettir thrust up with a spear and killed one man, but he could not rise from his knee by reason of his wound; the others leapt down and attacked him; young Illugi threw his shield over him and made defence for both in most manly wise.

Grettir killed another man, whose body fell upon him, so that he could not use his sword; wherefore Angle at that moment was able to stab him between the shoulders, and many another wound they gave him till they thought he was dead.

Angle took Grettir's short sword and struck at the head of the body with such force that a piece of the sword-blade was nicked out. So died Grettir, the bravest man of all who ever dwelt in Iceland.

*PRINTED IN GREAT BRITAIN BY THE UNIVERSITY PRESS, ABERDEEN*